BABY GOT
BACK

BABY GOT BACK
ANAL EROTICA

EDITED BY
RACHEL KRAMER BUSSEL

Published in the United States by Cleis Press, Inc., 2246 Sixth Street, Berkeley, California 94710.

Printed in the United States.
Cover design: Scott Idleman/Blink
Cover photograph: Tetra Images
Text design: Frank Wiedemann

First Edition.
10 9 8 7 6 5 4 3 2 1

Trade paper ISBN: 978-1-57344-962-5
E-book ISBN: 978-1-57344-975-5

Contents

INTRODUCTION: PREPARED FOR PLEASURE

Anal sex is an activity that doesn't "just happen." There needs to be at least some planning involved by one of the parties, preferably both (or all), an acknowledgment that something special is about to occur. The stories collected here feature various types of anal play, but in every case, preparation is a key part, both mentally and physically. For many of the characters you're about to encounter, the thrill of anticipation kickstarts their anal foreplay, sending them on a journey that often changes the course of their sex life.

Many of these twenty-three stories play with the taboo nature of anal sex, its forbidden quality that even its biggest fans still fixate on. We are often drawn to anal sex precisely because even now, in 2013, there's still a hint of exoticness to it. In these tales, men and women open themselves up, literally, to their lovers, sometimes for the first time. All parties learn about the specific thrills that make playing with that area so pleasurable. Sometimes a character has had a previous negative experience with anal exploration, like Lela in "Rectified," by Tiffany Reisz.

When Brad tells her, "I know what I'm doing," she's not sure if she can trust him, but she takes a chance. You'll have to read on to find out exactly how she's rewarded for her risk-taking.

Whether using fingers, tongues, toys like butt plugs (vibrating and not), anal beads or anal dilators, these men and women appreciate the pleasures that can be found when they relax, let go and open themselves up. Furthermore, anal sex doesn't have to be the only action going on; it can be combined with other kinds of touch. Here's what happens to Vanessa in "A Winter's Tail," by Veronica Wilde: "She sighed with pleasure, then surprise, as the tip of the anal beads eased into her ass. Oh god, yes; he was double-penetrating her with two toys. This was what she lived for. He gently pushed the beads inside her tightness, making her squirm, then slowly withdrew them until she cried from sheer delight." In "No Rest for the Sick," by Medea Mor, Becky experiences a kinky dual delight when Patrick delivers a firm, powerful spanking to her plugged bottom: "He followed quickly with two more hard slaps on her now-burning flesh. They reverberated through her body, hitting the plug in her ass before echoing off it again, making her squirm in his lap."

I feel responsible for telling you that if you're trying anal sex at home, lube is a must; these stories are here to entertain and arouse you, but if you'd like to learn more about how to approach real-life anal sex, read Tristan Taormino's *The Ultimate Guide to Anal Sex for Women*, Bill Brent's *The Ultimate Guide to Anal Sex for Men* and Karlyn Lotney's *The Ultimate Guide to Strap-On Sex*. Anal isn't about going as fast as you can, but about slowing down, unwinding, indulging in the process as much as the outcome. These characters take their time so they can enjoy every part of the process, from the first meandering touches, exploring a lover's "back door," to the more intense acts. I hope you enjoy the journeys these characters take and find plenty in here to turn you on.

Rachel Kramer Bussel
New York City

BRENDA'S BOOTY

Tenille Brown

It was a day at the shop just like any other. Hot, and Brenda was sweating with her cleaver in her hand, customers roaming in and out, placing orders and picking up their packages of meat.

She was brushing a short wisp of hair from her forehead when she noticed him standing there. The man stood just over six feet; he was standing there looking, but acting like he wasn't looking, which was what bothered her the most. He would be the last customer of the day if he would just get on with it, but he wouldn't. He wanted to gawk instead.

Brenda knew she could and probably should ask if she could help him, but she wasn't in the mood to play his game. She'd let him stand there and pretend he didn't know what he wanted, all the while ogling her ass in the tight jeans she wore today.

It took the man twelve damned minutes.

"Excuse me," he said, finally, "how might one go about getting a ham?"

And something went straight through Brenda. The eyeing

she could handle. The game playing she was used to. But he was at a meat shop for Christ's sake!

Brenda slammed the cleaver down on the counter and swung around. She looked the man square in the eye and said, "Kill a damn hog!"

And the man, medium in weight, with smooth brown skin and nice hair, had nerve enough to look surprised.

"Ma'am, I just want to order a ham," he said with nervous laughter.

Brenda exhaled. "Then say that. Hell, it's not rocket science."

Her eyes dared him to ask to see her boss. She was almost begging him to so she could tell him that *she* was her fucking boss, that *she* owned this place and she didn't answer to any damned body.

But the man only nodded and said, "Thank you, ma'am, and you have a nice day."

The thing was, though, being killed with kindness didn't fly with Brenda.

She called after him as he turned to walk out the door. "Hey!"

He turned around.

"You came in here for a damn ham. You're leaving with a damned ham. And I'm giving you the best I got...at a discount."

So Brenda picked him one, the biggest one, and placed it on the counter. "Now, will there be anything else for you today, *sir*?"

"Well," he said, leaning over the counter so that he was face-to-face with her. "My name is Lewis and I'd like to take your name and number, if you don't mind."

Brenda stood up straight. She posed just for a minute so that he could take it all in, big bust, small waist and all.

Then she said, "The number to the shop is right on the door. Maybe you missed it."

Lewis said, "Maybe you misunderstood. I don't want to call you here at your job. I want to call you at home. On your private line."

"I don't have a private line." Brenda turned around and let him get one last glimpse of her ass before he let himself out.

But when she heard the bell sound over the door, she realized he hadn't lingered.

"Hey!" Brenda called after him. "Lewis? That what you said your name was?"

Before he could confirm, Brenda picked up one of her business cards and scribbled her home number on the back of it. "Call me later or tomorrow or whenever and tell me how that ham was. I appreciate customer feedback."

"You're an ass man. How typical." Brenda sucked her teeth.

This was after Lewis had hugged her hello and *accidentally* let his hand slip lower than the small of her back.

The first time she let him touch her and her ass was what he went for. Greedy and impatient, like a kid.

"How typical of you to call me typical," Lewis said, blatantly and roughly rubbing her rump now through the cotton of her dress.

Brenda slapped at Lewis's hands. "Don't make me change my mind about getting in this car."

"No, don't do that. I have a whole thing planned, and that might just ruin it."

Lewis was smooth, and Brenda was almost tempted to say she had met her match. It was all new to her. She was perplexed.

He stopped flirting with her ass long enough to open the door of his convertible for her.

The drive was scenic and long, but the talk was stimulating. Brenda barely noticed that nearly two hours had passed before they reached their destination.

"A drive-in?" She cocked her head.

"And it ain't typical," Lewis affirmed.

Brenda took off her seat belt and glared up at the screen. "Well, it was in nineteen-sixty-five," she said.

Lewis removed his own seat belt and the belt around his jeans as well. "Then I want you to tell me if this is typical. Bring your slick-talking ass over here and have a seat on my lap."

If she were in her twenties, Brenda might have hesitated, but she was thirty-seven. She didn't have a three-month, three-week or even three-day rule. She could fuck whenever she felt good and goddamned ready.

And she was ready.

So, without a word, Brenda climbed on Lewis's lap. She lifted the skirt of her dress so that it flowed over both her legs and his. Lewis pushed his hands underneath and found the edge of her panties and slowly began pulling them down.

"We're not the only ones out here, you know," she said, as if she actually cared.

"But we'll be the only ones here fucking."

She got comfortable on his lap, pulling out Lewis's stiff rod and guiding it inside her. Brenda began riding Lewis slow and easy, using her wetness to her advantage, gliding down slowly, then rising up again.

She grabbed on to his small ears, leaning forward to smell the coconut conditioner he liked to use on his thick curly hair.

Brenda whispered, "Don't worry, baby. You can just tell me what the movie was about."

Lewis' thick cock sent wavelike sensations through Brenda's body. No longer satisfied with the slow and steady rhythm they had started out with, she began bouncing her large, rounded ass on his tight thighs.

Kissing him as they fucked in public, Brenda's eyes rolled back. And just when Brenda knew she was about to beat Lewis to the punch, just when she knew she was about to come, Lewis removed his cock and began rubbing it against her ass.

"Mmmm. You know I love it when you tease, baby," she said. "Now, give it back."

Lewis did give it back. At least he tried. He placed his cock a little farther back this time, toward her rear opening.

Brenda didn't speak at first. She didn't want to jump the gun when he might have only been playing around.

But then came the push and the pressure, and Brenda jumped what seemed like five feet in the air.

"Hold on, wait a minute," she said.

"What?" Lewis asked, confused.

"Take the needle off the damned record. You are not fucking me in the ass, man."

Lewis nodded slowly. "I get it. It might be a little soon. I'm sorry I rushed it."

"No, no, no. That's not what I mean, Lewis." Brenda was pulling her panties back up, now. And she was back in the passenger's seat looking Lewis straight in the eye.

"Baby, you have me a bit confused." Lewis said.

"Well, hell, I'll just say it. I don't do that. And the reason being is, I don't believe a dick belongs in anybody's ass."

"A simple no would have sufficed, Brenda."

"No, it wouldn't have. You would have wanted to know why. Men always want to know why." Brenda was shaking her head from side to side now, frustrated.

They always wanted it and went for it. That had been Brenda's experience. She couldn't help her ass. Her mama's ass was big. And so was her grandmama's. It was her blessing and her curse.

"So, you never...?" Lewis started.

"I didn't say I never. I actually have...once, twice with this one guy. And it wasn't anything to write home about. So, you can get that particular thing out of your damn head. Now pretty much anything else," Brenda said, before easing back onto his lap, "is on the table."

She didn't wait for him to answer before she again started to ride him, this time like he was a bucking bull, twisting and turning her hips in motions that held his mouth frozen open and his hands gripping the steering wheel.

She knew that when he came he would be vocal, so when Lewis began to buck, Brenda covered his mouth with hers and squeezed her hips as tight as she could as he came inside her.

She sat there a while slumped against his chest, sweat easing between her breasts. Brenda freed Lewis and let him catch his breath, and then she threw her leg over his lap and let him finger-fuck her for the next twenty minutes until she was jerking and convulsing herself.

Lewis licked his fingers one by one, nasty fellow that he was.

He was driving her back home before the credits rolled.

Brenda liked Lewis's cock better than any other. It was the perfect length and girth, and maybe it was silly of her to think so, but it seemed his was made for her.

Her cunt, though, not her ass.

And was it really wrong to be satisfied with just that? That Brenda actually liked lying on her back and spreading her legs wide for him? That she loved when Lewis slid his hands beneath her and lifted her ass off the mattress to bring her closer to him?

Thinking of these things, Brenda wiggled as he pulled the stretchy pair of pants over her bubble-shaped ass and wide hips.

Many men had tried and all had failed, except for Gary those two times. And he hadn't made it very appealing. He'd been too rushed and he came too quickly and really, Brenda didn't know what the fucking big deal was about it any damn way.

So, if Lewis was fine fucking the way that they were, then so was she.

Lewis was licking Brenda's cunt from behind. He loved the taste of her and he didn't mind saying so. He was kissing and sucking her shoulders now and making his way down her back.

But, this, Brenda wasn't expecting this. It was his tongue.

Then again, over the months, Lewis had given Brenda many things she didn't expect, like multiple orgasms. *That* was an unexpected and newfound pleasure.

But, yes, his tongue. His exceptionally long tongue had gone from lingering along the small of her back to slowly gliding along the hills of her asscheeks. Then he used the tip to slightly separate them and he put his tongue there, too.

"You taste lovely," Lewis paused long enough to say.

He was sucking and making little noises with his lips and his tongue and Brenda was soaking the couch beneath her. She was embarrassed and she wasn't. She wanted him to stop so she could gather her bearings. She wanted him to keep going so she could lose control.

Lewis's tongue was strong, strong enough to push against her opening just a little, just enough. And it didn't hurt or feel awkward or weird. Brenda actually liked it.

She liked the way his tongue loosened up the tightness. But just his tongue and that was all. He didn't need to go any farther because already her eyes were clenched tight and she was crawling up the couch cushions.

And she was coming, right there in her own living room and they hadn't gotten anywhere near fucking. Her body was trembling so much she thought it would never stop, but eventually it did, and Lewis was right there to turn her over, suck on her nipples and slip his cock inside of her.

The pomp and circumstance made Brenda giggle. Lewis was always up to something. Tonight it was oil and candles all over his two-bedroom apartment.

"I know how it is being on your feet all day. You could use a good rubdown," he had said when he opened the door for her.

Now, lying on a quilt in the middle of his living room, the words floated in circles around her ears.

A man could get lost in that ass...

And as he massaged her body with his strong, rough hands, all she could think was how she wanted him to get lost, so lost in her ass.

Lewis began with his finger first, entering slowly. She barely felt the pressure at first, and then it was more intense.

Curious and amazed at the motions Lewis could make with one digit, then two, Brenda lay still, awaiting what was next.

He was hovering over her.

"Is this okay?" he asked, finger-fucking her ass.

Brenda nodded, her mouth parted open.

Then she felt the first, then second ridges of his fingers. He turned them in half circles and pushed them in deeper.

Brenda opened like a bud, and she found herself lifting her hips from the floor to meet his fingers, to help him go deeper.

"Lost," Lewis said, "Completely lost."

But Brenda was already lost. She pounded her fists on the

floor as she stained the quilt. She came down flat and hard, bringing Lewis down on top of her.

She might have slept there had Lewis not tapped her on the shoulder.

"Get up, babe," he said, "I made you a ham sandwich."

"What? No treat tonight?" Brenda stood up and stepped back with her hands on her hips.

This was after Lewis had done everything from licking her toes and fingers to sucking on her clit until it was sore. He had laid her across the kitchen table and covered her with honey and removed that with his tongue, as well.

"Treat? I thought I was the treat, my dear?" Lewis bowed at the waist dramatically, naked as a jaybird.

"Funny, but you know what I mean."

Lewis stepped up close to Brenda, then reached around and grabbed onto her ass. "Someone wants their booty toyed with, eh?"

"I have to ask for it, do I?" Brenda pretended to pout.

"You want it finger-fucked some more? Want me to lick it?"

Brenda shook her head. She lowered her chin in her hands. "I was thinking we could try something else."

Lewis held up a finger. "Ah! That little dildo you keep in your nightstand you thought I didn't know about. We can try that tonight."

Brenda stomped her feet. "You know damn well what the hell I'm talking about, Lewis."

Lewis kissed Brenda on her neck and tweaked her nipple. "Darling, you told me in the beginning. Cocks aren't made for asses. And I respect that."

Brenda folded her arms. "Fuck your respect." And she turned and left Lewis standing alone in the kitchen.

* * *

Brenda normally didn't mind being awakened in the middle of the night, but she was pissed. Lewis snuck up behind her and wrapped his arms around her waist. She slapped his hands away.

"Go to sleep," she said.

But he was pulling her nightgown up above her knees.

"I'm not sleepy," he said.

"I am. And I've got work in the morning."

"I've got work right now. And it's right underneath this gown."

His hands were there before he finished speaking and he was rubbing right between her fleshy cheeks. There was something on his hands, but Brenda was too distracted to ask what it was.

As if reading her mind, Lewis said, "Don't worry, it'll help, because I do realize, my dear, that an asshole is *not* a cunt by any means."

Lewis straddled Brenda, his knees on either side of her hips. He lowered himself down on top of her, sighing.

"You feel as nice as I thought you would," he said.

But Brenda knew he couldn't see the smile that was spreading across the face buried in the pillows.

The tip of Lewis's cock felt much different from the tip of his tongue and much, much different from the tip of his finger. There was width and there was weight, there was guidance and there was determination.

He distracted her with a tongue in her ear and a hand cupping her breast, all the while whispering dirty, nasty things to her.

"I've been waiting to get lost in this ass."

The nastier he talked, the wetter Brenda became.

She began to finger herself as Lewis moved slowly and carefully inside her ass.

"Fuck me," Brenda uttered against the wet and wrinkled sheets.

"Yes," Lewis breathed. "But I don't want to come too soon. And I don't want to hurt that big, pretty ass of yours."

Brenda's fingers were drenched. She pressed back against Lewis's solid crotch as he pushed carefully forward, opening her wider with every thrust.

When finally she could hold back no longer, Brenda came first, tossing her head back into Lewis's hairless chest.

Lewis continued, now gripping Brenda's cheeks and squeezing them together against his cock.

He became rigid as a log against her back, releasing from the base of his throat the must guttural moan Brenda had ever heard.

"Hold still, Brenda," Lewis said. "Here it comes."

And it was different, receiving come inside her ass, different but good and Brenda lay there in the wetness with Lewis slumped on top of her breathing heavily.

"Think you can find your way out?" she asked, looking back over her shoulder and winking.

Lewis grinned. "I don't know if I want to."

RECTIFIED

Tiffany Reisz

The Butterfly.

Cowgirl.

Missionary.

Doggie.

Lela flipped page after page after page in the sex-position manual and grew more and more depressed with every picture that greeted her. All of them. She'd done every single position in the book.

Tears of frustration burned her eyes. She blinked rapidly to dispel them, but one escaped and landed in the center of a Lotus position sex diagram.

"Dammit." She hastily wiped off the tear, but it had already left a water mark. Now she had to buy the stupid thing.

"I've seen women crying into books before, but usually it's over in the fiction section," came a voice from behind her.

Turning around, Lela came face to chest with a man over six feet tall. Craning her neck, she found his face rather closer to the ceiling than her own and discovered that it was a handsome face and the man was smiling kindly at her.

"The nonfiction is depressing enough for me."

The man cocked his head to the side and gave her a searching look. She should have been embarrassed getting caught by a man as she wept into a sex-position manual. But after spending an hour in stirrups today as a parade of doctors prodded her vagina, cervix and uterus, the tattered remains of her dignity had packed their bags and headed west.

He coughed softly and Lela noticed he'd extended his hand. Quickly pulling herself together, she tucked the book under her arm and shook his hand.

"Brad."

"Lela. I'm a mess." She found his grip oddly comforting and didn't pull her fingers back from him.

"Hi, Lela. Are you going to tell me what's wrong or do I have to spend the rest of my life wondering why a beautiful woman was weeping over *101 Perfect Nights*? I mean, it's no Kama Sutra, but it has a happy ending. Lots of them."

He meant the words as a joke but Lela couldn't laugh.

"No happy ending for me." She leaned tiredly against the bookcase.

Brad squeezed her hand a little tighter. She should have been scared of a man so big, built like a football player, dressed like a stock trader and hanging out in the sex section of a bookstore. But something in his eyes made her trust him a little, and she needed to talk, had to talk. A stranger seemed better suited than a friend.

"No happy ending?" Brad crossed his arms over his broad chest. He had salt-and-pepper hair but looked no more than forty. "Every story should have a happy ending. Well, any story that has you in a bed in it."

"You're hitting on me." Lela smiled for the first time today.

"I'm flirting with you. I have the floggers back home

when you want me to hit on you."

Lela raised an eyebrow at him. God, it would be nice to just spend a day in bed with a man like this—sexy, confident, and kinky, too. But she knew it would end the way it always ended.

Pain. Tears. Apologies.

"I appreciate it. My ego needs all the help it can get. But I promise, I would be a waste of effort."

"I refuse to believe that, Lela. Tell me what's wrong. If you're not going to flirt back, the least you can do for *my* ego is to tell me why."

She wrinkled up her face in embarrassment.

"It's gross."

"Time of the month? Not gross. Easy to work around."

"If only. I..." she began and paused, deciding if she really wanted to be one of those people who told her life story to a stranger. Yes was the answer. Today. Yes. "I have severe endometriosis. I am twenty-seven years old and have been trying to have sex for ten years. Never had it without pain. And today the doctors—a whole team of them—stuck their fingers in me and said surgery was the only way to rectify things. Why have surgery to have good sex if I've never had good sex and don't even know if it's worth it?"

Brad brought her hand to his lips for a quick kiss.

"That is a sad story. So what's the book for?"

"This? They said I should try some different positions. I don't think they believed me when I told them I've tried them all."

"Anal?"

She nodded. "A couple times in college. Didn't go well."

"Did it hurt?"

"He didn't know what he was doing. Another fail."

"I don't know if this will convince you to stop crying into sex books and come back to my place with me but..."

"But what?" She let him pull her closer, close enough she could smell the cedar scent of his soap and see the smile that lurked at the corner of his lips.

"But...I know what I'm doing." He said the words with confidence bordering on arrogance and with such an intimate gleam in his eyes that Lela couldn't stem the tide of images his words conjured. The thought of a man inside her without her body seizing with pain?

"I've never gone to bed with a man I just met."

"No wonder you're crying in the bookstore."

"You won't think less of me?" She smiled at him.

"The only women I judge for their sexual choices are the women who turn me down. All none of them."

"I'd hate to break your streak."

"Then don't."

"It probably won't work, you know? I'm warning you right now."

"I'll probably have you screaming from pleasure in under an hour. I'm warning you right now. Say yes."

Lela laughed. Might as well. It was the least she could do for her poor vagina after all she'd put it through today.

"Yes."

"Good. Let's go."

"I have to buy this first. I got it wet."

"Trust me. Female tears are the least of the body fluids on this book." He took it and shoved it onto the shelf while Lela made a mental note to wash her hands thoroughly at Brad's place.

They grabbed a taxi and spent the twenty-minute ride whispering abbreviated life stories to each other. Lela Moore, well-paid actuary, single, no kids, no hope. Brad Wolfe—he swore it was his real name—ex-wife, no kids, just a club he treated like his baby.

"What kind of club?"

"The best kind," he said and gave her a wolfish smile.

The club turned out to be exactly what she'd imagined. Black walls, ornate staircases, many rooms with closed doors.

"Sex club?" she asked as he escorted her inside.

"Kink club. We cater to all the fetishes here."

"Is 'terrified of sex' a fetish?"

"It's a damn shame, is what that is." Brad led her up the central staircase to a room at the end of a second-floor hallway. He opened the door to a bedroom that appeared to have been lifted from a nineteenth-century house of ill repute. Seemed an appropriate setting for some behavior of ill repute. "Let's get you over that, shall we?"

"If you can do it, you're a miracle worker."

"I can do it if you'll let me. You've gotta trust me though." He opened an ebony cabinet inlaid with ivory and pulled out a flogger.

"Okay, you weren't kidding about the flogging thing?"

"I never kid about floggings. You say you're afraid of pain during sex. Fine. Let's get the pain out of the way first so you can focus on the sex."

"Are you—"

Brad strode to Lela and looked down at her. The move emphasized the height disparity. She wasn't short. Not at all. But he was so big she felt tiny in comparison and rather hated to admit how much she liked that.

"Lela...I know...what...I...am doing..." He said each word slowly and punctuated the sentence with a kiss. A long kiss, a slow kiss, a deep kiss that said even more than his words that he knew what he was doing.

"I believe you."

"Good. Take your clothes off."

She almost balked at the order before deciding she'd already come this far. What was stopping her? Off came her high heels, her skirt, blouse and bra.

"No panties?" Brad asked as she stood before him naked.

"I took them off at the doctor's office. Didn't put them back on again. I'm soaked with lube."

"A woman who comes pre-lubed? Love it."

Brad ran his hands up and down her arms. He touched her back, belly and hips before cupping her breasts. He teased her nipples with his fingertips as he assaulted her mouth with the softest of kisses. The first stirrings of desire danced in her stomach. She'd been here before. The foreplay, the buildup, the hunger and need...and then wrenching pain and crushing disappointment. But maybe she could let go of her fears enough to at least enjoy the prelude to the disaster.

"Come here. Right here." He pulled her to the side of the bed and gave her one more kiss before pushing her onto her stomach. She tried to relax into the soft silk sheets as Brad adjusted the width of her feet still on the floor. She heard something like the clinking of metal and then felt something wrap around her ankles. Her legs were locked in, immobile.

"Brad?"

"Spreader bar."

"I can't move my legs."

"You're naked. Where were you planning on going?"

"Good point."

"Question. You said the last time you had anal sex was...?"

"College. Five years ago."

"I'm not small."

"I noticed."

"Stay here."

"Very funny," she said as she tried again to move her legs.

She heard him rummaging through the cabinet and in seconds he'd returned to her.

"I need to open you up a little so I don't hurt going in. You still believe I know what I'm doing?"

"Yes. I think."

"Good enough." Brad dropped to his knees behind her, spread her cheeks open and started to lick her.

"Wait…"

He pulled back.

"That 'wait' sounded like a 'wait, what the fuck are you doing' kind of 'wait.' I thought we already established—"

"Sorry. I just wasn't prepared for…you know."

"My tongue in your ass? Now you're prepared."

He started to lick her again and after a minute she started to relax. Before her doctor's appointment this morning she'd shaved and groomed thoroughly. And if she could admit it to herself, it did feel weirdly good. Brad massaged her thighs while he kissed her and slipped a hand between her legs. He slid one finger into her vagina as he pushed his tongue inside her. A moan escaped her throat. The doctors had told her to experiment with positions more. Maybe she'd call them tomorrow and tell them that she'd done her homework.

"Do fingers hurt?"

"No," she said, panting. "Fingers usually don't. Just—"

"Cocks?"

"Yeah."

"Please try not to sound depressed when I'm massaging your G-spot."

She laughed into the sheets. "Sorry about that."

Brad bit down hard on her right cheek and she gasped with the sudden pain.

"You have an amazing ass. That's not the only time I'm

going to bite it today."

"Thanks for the warning," she said, still gasping.

"Another warning, I'm going to thoroughly lube you right now and insert a plug. It'll open you up."

"You don't ask permission to do things, I'm starting to notice. You just do them."

"Now you're catching on."

Brad started to ply her with the cold liquid, moving slowly inside her, one finger and eventually two. Before long she started to feel something she hadn't quite expected—pleasure. Intense pleasure. His wet fingers deep in her, his free hand massaging her back, bottom and thighs, his words of encouragement as she opened up to him, they set every nerve in the lower half of her body alight.

"Good girl," Brad whispered as she moaned and dug her fingers into the sheets.

"Thought I was being bad here."

"Oh no. We don't play by those rules in this house. Any beautiful woman who spreads for me on a Monday morning? She's a very good girl."

Brad pulled his fingers out and Lela winced as he pushed the plug into her. It fit snugly but if she forced herself to relax, it didn't hurt at all. She felt a fullness from it, a pleasant penetration. She made a mental note to never try anal with a guy who didn't know what he was doing ever again.

She sensed Brad kneeling down again and unbuckling her from the spreader bar.

"I'm going to flog you. I have two very good reasons for doing that. My erection is just one of those reasons."

He pushed his hips into her bottom and she felt the truth of his words against her skin.

"Do I get to know the other reason?"

"Endorphins. Intercourse causes you pain. Endorphins fight pain. I flog you and the endorphins start flooding your system. It's all very scientific."

"That's why we're doing it?"

"That and reason one." He pressed reason one into her hip again.

He turned her to face him and wrapped a silk scarf around her wrists. As he tied her wrists, she watched his face. He seemed utterly absorbed in the task and his dark eyes shone with intelligence mixed with desire. Without warning, she kissed him. He didn't object.

"I'm still going to flog you," he said when he pulled back from the kiss.

"I wasn't trying to stop you."

"I like you, Lela. I might have to fuck you all day."

"If you manage to pull this off without me in agony, I'll let you."

"Let me? Not sure I asked." He gave her a wink and spun her to the bedpost where he quickly tied her arms above her head.

Lela closed her eyes and took a deep breath, a breath that she released in a yelp as the flogger hit the center of her back. Brad took aim and hit her again. Up and down her entire back, from her neck to her knees, he flogged her. It hurt but not badly enough that she needed him to stop. Every blow set her skin burning and her body flinching even as the plug inside her sent shivers of pleasure through her hips.

The flogging ended after a few minutes, and Brad pushed his body into her back.

"I'd flog your beautiful body all day, but my cock won't let me."

"A firm taskmaster, is he?"

"I try never to tell him no."

Brad untied her wrists from the bedpost and swept her up in his arms. The sudden removal of her feet from the floor set her laughing even as he laid her in the center of the bed.

"Don't laugh. I'm trying to be sexy."

"You are sexy, Brad." She gripped him by the back of his neck as he sucked her nipples one by one. "You don't have to try."

"Now tell me, what position do you most wish you could do without pain?"

"All of them," she said, and he gave her a steely stare. "Okay. There's a version of missionary where her legs are up on his thighs. Always thought that looked so sexy spreading like that, ankles on opposite sides of the room."

"Nice. You can do that position in anal."

Brad sat up on his knees and unbuttoned his shirt. She watched him undress, adoring every square inch of his thick, muscled body. He hadn't been kidding about the "big" part either, she noted as he rolled a condom onto his length.

"Knees to chest," he ordered and she complied. He worked the plug out of her and sat it on the bedside table. It shocked her how big it was. If that fit into her comfortably, so should he. Picking up the tube of lube again, he worked even more of it into her before slathering a generous amount over his cock. He dried his hands, grabbed her thighs and yanked her close. Lela stared up at the ceiling as he positioned himself and started to push inside her. Inch by inch he worked his way in with slow, short thrusts. When her body gave him no resistance, he sunk deep and lay on top of her. As his hips settled between her thighs, her legs spread even farther apart.

"Good?" He bit her neck.

"Very good," she breathed. Very good...she meant it. He was inside her, all of him, moving, thrusting, fucking her. She couldn't believe that a man was inside her and she felt nothing but wanton pleasure. Brad put a hand to the side of her head to hold himself up as he reached between their bodies and found her clitoris. With each slow deep thrust, he rubbed the swollen knot. Her hips rocked into his. She couldn't get enough of his cock, his fingers, his mouth on her face, her neck. All these years, this is what she'd been missing.

Lela's body started to tighten. Her shoulders came off the bed and she buried her head against Brad's chest as her vagina clenched and her whole body shook with the climax she'd never experienced during sex before. Collapsing against the bed, she merely breathed as Brad pumped into her until his eyes shut tight and he came with a hoarse grunt.

Carefully, he pulled out of her and lay on his back. Laughing, Lela crawled on top of him and stretched out across his chest.

"Verdict?" An arrogant grin decorated his lips.

"Verdict is...you totally know what you're doing."

Brad pulled her close for a kiss. The smile left his face.

"And?" She saw the question in his eyes.

"And...sex is amazing. I'm having the surgery."

"Good. Hurry up and schedule it so I can fuck your pussy in every position that's ever made you cry."

"That would be all of them."

"Then the sooner the better."

"How about now? My ass can take it."

"Now..." he said, as he pulled her into Lotus position and grabbed the lube again, "would be perfect."

DELIVERY

Emerald

I knew I wouldn't get to see Wesley much, if at all, while we were in Vegas. Our overlapping time there would only be about fourteen hours, and he would be busy with the conference during the day, while I was committed to plans with my sisters in the evening.

Still, that didn't make it any less of a delicious coincidence that we were going to be there at the same time. I grinned as I watched the myriad billboards fly by on my ride from the airport to the Strip. It was Thursday afternoon, and my flight from Hartford had just landed. I had a couple of hours to get to my hotel room and settle in before my three older sisters arrived for the extended bachelorette party weekend for my next-older sister, Julia.

Wesley had been in Las Vegas since Monday for an IT conference, where his company was presenting the product rollout he'd been overseeing for months. The distance from Boston, where he was a vice president of software development, to where I lived in western Massachusetts usually limited our in-person meetings to once a week or so, but rollout preparation had kept his department so busy lately that we hadn't seen each other in more than three weeks.

Realistically, I knew there would be no sneaking away from my own plans tonight: my sister was the reason we were all gathering here, and it would be inexcusable for me to back out of any of her bachelorette festivities no matter how much I wanted to get laid. And in order to keep up with the launch schedule back home, Wesley would have to leave for the airport around five the next morning. Regardless, remote as it was, just the possibility of a rendezvous in my favorite city set off a tingle of giddiness in me.

Our bachelorette quartet was staying at the Venetian. The cab dropped me off, and I swished through the revolving doors out of the baking heat and into the elegant, high-ceilinged lobby. Like many front lobbies of the extravagant hotels on the Strip, it held a muted air of elegance and sophistication. Underneath it, however, ran the unmistakable current of the decadence and hedonism Sin City's reputation promised—and which it did its best to deliver.

I dropped my suitcase on the bed in the room I'd be sharing with Julia and started to search for my bikini. I figured I'd hang out at the pool until my oldest sister, Claire, arrived in an hour, followed by Gloria shortly thereafter and finally Julia early in the evening. The four of us had an eight o'clock dinner reservation.

I took the elevator down to the pool level, my eyes automatically peeled for a glimpse of Wesley. I giggled at my silliness. He wouldn't be wandering around the Venetian—most likely he was in the middle of a session at the Mandalay Bay where the conference was held and where he was staying. As I stepped outside, I felt my beach bag vibrate and reached inside for my phone.

Wesley had text messaged. *Session break. You here yet?*

I pranced to the nearest open chaise lounge to drop my bag and shed my cover-up before pushing REPLY. *Yes—at Venetian pool.* I reached for my sunscreen and was reapplying it to my thighs when the phone buzzed again.

Conference over in an hour but have to network till dinner. Going to the Delmonico tonight.

I blinked as I read the words on the little glowing screen. The Delmonico was the elegant steakhouse of Emeril Lagasse located in the Venetian. A slow smile formed on my face, and my heart started to pound as I pushed REPLY. *So are we.*

A few minutes before eight, my sisters and I sat in the posh lounge of the Delmonico waiting to be seated. Wesley had contacted me after the conference to inform me that their reservation was for seven thirty and that he would be with a group of colleagues.

"Lynn, did you pick up the show tickets for tonight?" Gloria's question brought my attention back to the immediate vicinity.

"Yeah, we're all set," I answered. I fiddled with my drink and adjusted a strap of my dress. I had chosen a short, shimmery black cocktail dress with a draped neck and wide straps. Simple on top. On the bottom, however, were the boots. White patent leather with black crisscrossing stripes, up to the knee, they turned the simple little-black-dress look into something with the Sin City-esque edge I was looking for. I topped it off with white wrist-length gloves and my hair in a French twist.

"So what are we seeing tonight?" Julia asked. While she had picked the weekend we would be here, the rest of us had handled all the weekend's scheduling and arrangements, some of which were a surprise for the bride.

Claire laughed. "Just because we're in Vegas now doesn't

mean you get to know yet. You'll find out when we get there."

I smiled. I suspected Julia would enjoy the cadre of male strippers we were taking her to see, though she would probably have been too shy to admit she was interested in going. All the more convenient that she had the three of us to plan it for her.

The host approached us, and I picked up my black clutch and gestured for my sisters to go ahead as we filed behind him and entered the dining area. I spotted Wesley immediately, seated at a long table of about ten people. I didn't look back as we passed through a wide doorway into a larger, open dining area, but I knew Wesley had seen me. The host led us halfway through the room and stopped beside our table against the wall. I waited for my sisters to sit down and then slipped into the outside seat on the plush bench that faced out into the dining room. I knew this was important.

From where I now sat, I could just barely see the section of the table in the next room where Wesley was sitting. As my sisters discussed the menu, I watched out of the corner of my eye as he spoke with the gentleman beside him, pausing once in a while to sip his drink. He looked dashing in his full black suit with black shirt and silver tie, and I couldn't help squirming a bit in my seat.

"What are you getting, Lynn?"

I turned my attention back to our table and scanned the elegant pages in front of me, figuring there was no point in spending the entire meal trying to watch what was happening in the next room. I offered Julia an answer just as our server arrived. We busied ourselves ordering for a few moments, and I handed my menu to the tuxedo-clad gentleman and tuned in to the conversation around me.

Until out of the corner of my eye, I saw Wesley get up from his table. I watched covertly as he set his napkin on his chair and excused himself. Then he turned and strode through the large doorway into our room, passing by with nary a glance at me as he disappeared down the hallway that led to the restroom.

That was my cue. Subtly, I slid my hand up my dress and gripped one side of my thong, sliding it down a few inches before reaching for the other side, alternately slipping it lower ever so slowly so as not to evidence what I was doing. Once it was past my knees, I worked it over one ankle and then the other with the pointed toes of my boots. Reaching under the table, I snapped it up and slipped it into my handbag, all the while responding to my sisters with nods and murmurs at the appropriate times.

After a few seconds, I excused myself and stood up, heading for the hallway across the room. The heels of my boots clicked on the marble floor as I entered and headed down the dim passageway. I could see through the shadows that there was no one at the end of it, so Wesley must have ducked into the men's room.

As I approached that door, it opened. Wesley stood leaning against the door frame, looking me up and down for an instant before opening it farther and backing up to let me in.

I entered into his hard kiss before the door was even shut, Wesley gripping my waist with one hand as he flipped the lock on the door with the other. Then he plunged both hands up my dress, pushing me back against the cool counter. I held myself away from him, aware that I was wet enough to make a mess on his black suit, but he grabbed my ass and gave it a hard smack, promptly earning my uncontrolled press against his body. I ground myself against him as he spanked me twice more, making me push harder into him each time. By then I was panting in his ear, feeling the hard cock beneath his pants against my bare skin.

I pulled away and looked down. "We made a mess," I whispered breathlessly.

"I imagine," he said without following my gaze. Instead he reached up and pulled the top of my dress down, exposing my tits and lowering his mouth to one nipple as his fingers found their way to my pussy. I knew we didn't have much time, however, and I knew exactly how I wanted to spend it. I backed up and pulled a condom and a tiny bottle of lube from my clutch.

He looked at it, then me. There was only one thing we used lube for.

"I want you to fuck my ass," I whispered as I handed them to him. Wesley inhaled sharply, and I placed a hand on his zipper. He was faster than I was, however, and had already ripped his belt open and grabbed the condom by the time I had his zipper halfway down. In seconds, his cock was sheathed and lubed, and I turned around and bent over the counter, wiggling in anticipation.

Gently, Wesley began to push his way in. I could feel his restraint, and a tiny moan pulsed from my throat as he slowly buried himself in me.

"Don't forget we don't have much time, sweetheart—don't hold back now." My tone was already breathless as I winked at him in the mirror.

Wesley hissed and dug his fingers into my hips, increasing his speed until he was pounding my ass with abandon, delivering intermittent smacks with each hand until I felt my pussy drip against the insides of my thighs. When his fingers snaked around and found my clit, I almost cried out. Biting my lip, I spread my legs wider as Wesley fucked me and fingered me at the same time.

The view of us in the mirror tipped me over the edge, and I gripped the sides of the sink as I held back a scream, orgasm jolting through me as Wesley's fingers held their position. I had barely finished when I saw Wesley's eyes close in the mirror, and his body jerked as he grabbed my hips and held me against him, breath pulsing as he emptied himself inside me.

We stood that way for a few seconds, trying to catch our breath. Then he pulled out slowly, and our movements turned hurried as we started to clean up. Wesley's eyes met mine in the mirror.

"You look gorgeous, by the way," he said.

I let out a muted laugh. "Maybe before you ravished me!" I began maneuvering numerous stray hairs back into place.

"You did then, too. But even more so now." Wesley dried his hands and slipped a hand gently into my hair as he kissed me. "It's good to see you," he said with a smile.

I smiled back. "You too, baby. You'd better get going."

He looked me up and down and nodded, rebuttoning his jacket. Then he stood for a moment, his gaze lingering, and leaned in to give me a final kiss before turning and slipping through the exit. I opened my clutch and pulled out my thong, a glance at my watch reassuring me that I hadn't been gone an unavoidably conspicuous amount of time.

I reentered the dining room, panties back in place, and slipped into my seat. The conversation seemed to have continued as though I had never left, and my sisters barely glanced up as I sat down. I stole a glance at Wesley's table. It looked almost identical to the way it had when I first saw it, Wesley talking with the person to his right as he held his tumbler and nodded at whatever the gentleman was saying. The only differences now were the remnants of my arousal all over Wesley's formerly impeccable black suit and the vague sting of bright-red handprints that still lingered on my ass.

Sin City, indeed.

MY TURN

Anya Levin

He'd love it, I can tell," Steph drawled, her fingernails dancing around the stem of her martini glass, flashes of neon in the shadows of the room.

"Stop it," I laughed, taking a healthy swallow of my own drink and hoping that the embarrassment I felt burning up my cheeks wasn't as obvious as I thought it was.

"Mark my words," Steph continued, her eyes shifting to the kitchen door James had just exited through to renew our drinks. "That man would be putty in your hands." Her eyes flashed to mine. "Sure you don't want me to break him in for you?"

Since Steph knew very well that there was no way I was going to share my latest flame, I just rolled my eyes at the question. The whole discussion had me jittery, not just the subject—though talking of backdoor pleasures wasn't something I did every day—but the intimacy of it. Steph loved crossing boundaries, but she'd never dragged my partners into her conversation so explicitly before. I didn't know if I was supposed to be flattered or offended.

A hand settled on my shoulder, squeezed, and I looked up in James's face just as he set another glass in front of me and slid into his own chair. For a moment he looked alien, all planes and sharp edges. The glasses perched on his nose did nothing to ease that impression.

His smile broke the seeming gulf between us, returning normality in a rush.

I smiled back and turned to face the room, staring unseeing over the familiar walls and decorations. I knew Steph didn't expect a response, which was good, because I didn't have one.

A buzzer sounded from the kitchen. I lifted my drink and cocked an eyebrow, smiling. "I think that's our dinner."

I walked from the room with slow, measured steps, James's arm around my waist in a supportive, comforting hug.

I felt like I had just escaped an interrogation.

The conversation came back to haunt me that night as James kissed me deeply, thoroughly, then effortlessly flipped me onto my knees. Ass in the air, from behind, doggie style; however you termed it, he loved it.

His fingers slid into my cunt with ease, then teased their way out slowly and danced up to my asshole and drew circles of my own wetness there.

"Umm," he said throatily, one fingertip just sliding inside. Gently, lovingly. He probed deeper, opening me up. The fullness made my cunt feel empty and needing and I bucked into his hand, wanting him to fill me where I needed to be filled.

Instead of his cock sliding against me, I felt his warm breath, then his lips just touching my butt. He peppered kisses across the surface of my ass, around the cheeks, across my tailbone and finally down between my cheeks. His lips finally landed squarely there—right in the middle. It felt loving and dirty at the same time, something I'd never been able to reconcile.

"Okay, enough," I said, turning under his hands and taking charge of the situation. I pushed him onto his back and climbed on, sliding him deep inside before he could argue. The ear-to-ear grin on his face said he didn't really care that I'd interrupted his meandering exploration, and then all thought was gone as everything came together and I came apart.

Later, as we lay in bed, I found I couldn't sleep. Sometimes it happened that way—drinks, friends, a quiet night, even a bone-shattering orgasm and I still couldn't get there.

"Do you ever want me to do that to you?"

James was half-asleep, splayed across the bed like a sacrificial victim of my demanding lust. I curled against his shoulder, breathing in his scent—sweat and soap and something undefinable that was just him. I was enjoying that so much that it took me a long minute to realize that he wasn't half-drowsing anymore.

"Sometimes," he said finally. Almost cautiously.

I slipped away from his warmth, my world somehow rocking on its foundation. I'd thought we'd done everything we wanted, that we'd ironed out the kinks and that both of us had everything we wanted from our sexual relationship.

Apparently not.

"Do you ever want more? Like a real..." I didn't know how to finish the sentence, didn't know if I wanted to.

He sat up with a heaving sigh, pushing his hair out of his face and then peering at me in the darkness. I saw the whites of his eyes, imagined I saw the blue that lay inside those white rings.

"It's not a big deal," he said. "Really." He leaned forward, kissed me smack on the lips and then flopped back down to sleep.

I wished I could dismiss it as easily as he seemingly did, but I couldn't. So I did something about it. I researched. I shopped.

I didn't ask Steph about it.

Predictably, I even chickened out a few times.

Until we got hot and heavy one night. Something mindless was on TV and we'd moved on from its illuminated pincers. James had avoided my ass for what seemed like weeks, keeping to more traditional activities. I'd enjoyed it, and I was pretty sure he'd enjoyed it, but given that his interest in my butt had long been relegated in my mind to more of a fascination, I found that every time he detoured around or away, guilt rested even more heavily on my shoulders.

We'd started with the obligatory teasing touches and moved into naked and hands at play, and then he started cruising down the front of me until he landed mouth-first on my cunt. I propped myself on my elbows to watch him, because I loved to watch him. He pulled my thighs apart and seemed to settle there, and everything would have been fine but he stuttered. Not verbally, but his fingers seemed to tremble and run away, as if shy, as he grasped my asscheeks to pull me against him. His fingertips just brushed between them and then they were gone, leaving me to wonder if I'd imagined the touch.

But I saw his face, and I saw the red that just touched his cheekbones, and the look in his eyes, and that was that.

I crawled out from underneath him, headed to the closet, and dug out my illicit purchases. They'd been shoved to the back of the closet more so it would be a surprise, not from embarrassment. Not that I was going to deny that I was embarrassed, a bit, at what I had planned. It wouldn't matter—couldn't matter—if he enjoyed it. If I fulfilled a desire, or more—a craving.

I picked two things, twisting the rest back into their papers and plastics and closing the box on them.

He had sat up, head back against the pillows, covers tucked tight against him. When I came back in the room, letting the plug and lube fall against the bed, he opened his eyes slowly. He didn't even look at what I'd retrieved, just pulled me into his arms and against him.

"I hate that it's weird," he said. "I don't want it to be weird."

"Neither do I," I said. "But I think we can fix it."

"Yes, I like your ass," he said, sliding his hands down to my posterior. "I'm sorry if that's weird to you, but I want to look at it, want to touch it, want to," his fingers slid against my asshole and I sucked in a breath at the surprise of the move, "fuck it."

"That's fine," I said, knowing that this time the red that surged through my cheeks wasn't something that could go unnoticed.

He paused, finger still lodged between my cheeks, warm and firm. His fingertip tapped that puckered hole, then he pulled his hand away entirely.

"Really?" he asked, face changing as the focus shifted from the more theoretical aspects of our relationship to a definitive physical intersection. He sat up, covers falling away as he pushed me onto my back and thrust my knees into the air, eyes locked on my nether regions.

I shifted to brace myself, and my arm hit the cold lube bottle, reminding me that I'd had other plans for the night.

"Hold on," I said, shifting my hips to break his attention,

intent on my own nefarious schemes, but he ignored my attempts to free myself, fingers simply tightening. He didn't touch me, didn't thrust a tongue or a finger into me, simply looked his fill and let his heated breath caress me. It was those moments that told me he didn't just like my ass, that he didn't just want to touch it and play with that, that the ass, *my* ass, right now, utterly fascinated him in a way that I couldn't relate to except to think of how I felt some mornings when I lay in bed, admiring the stretch and the length of his muscles as he slept. And even then, I had no desire to fuck his muscles, but he'd definitely said he wanted to fuck my ass. I couldn't really match that.

But I was damn well going to take a good, close look—and feel—of his ass, and I wasn't going to put it off any longer.

He moved when I yanked his hair, mouth forming a sound of pain that didn't go anywhere when his gaze hit the shiny black plug I was holding. It was smaller than I'd imagined, but I didn't think it had to be big to have a huge impact back there.

"You bought this?" He took the plug, sitting back on his heels.

Not quite where I wanted him, but close.

I grabbed the lube while he was focused on the plug, fiddled with the top, got it open.

He was turning the plug in his hands, feeling the weight of it, maybe imagining me before him, spread to receive it.

Little did he know.

"Thank you," I said, plucking the plug from his grasping fingers. I held it, trying to figure out how I was going to lube it up with only two hands.

"Hey!" He turned, something in his face reminding me of a little boy whose toy had been taken from him, and the idea was arousing. Desire he'd stoked before my preemptory pause flickered to life from its slow smolder, and the almost detached interest I'd had in the butt plug suddenly became something heavier, more weighty. I could imagine the heft of the plug in my own ass, the width of it pushing into me, opening me, and I decided then and there that I was going to be experiencing that particular treat as well, in the future.

For now…

"Turn," I said. I put the lube and the plug aside, wanting more than just to perpetrate an anal invasion. I wanted to learn him, to see him, maybe even the way he saw me.

Looking quizzical, he turned his back on me and sat there, shoulders tense, butt resting on muscled calves. I prodded his back with my fist, urging him to lean forward and show me the goods. He turned and caught my eye. "Are you sure about this?"

"Couldn't be more sure." And though it might not have been true when I'd gotten up the courage to scamper into the closet and retrieve my booty, it was now. Now I burned to see him, to feel him. I wanted to know the secrets of this type of pleasure and to share his desire.

He bent, and immediately I was aware of the intense vulnerability of his position, the naked revelation there. Revelation that I'd felt vaguely as I'd lain before him, ass high, but never so much as I did now, facing his cheeks and the dangling of his equipment, barely seen behind his thighs.

I started with a slow touch, my fingers on his back, and he shivered in response but kept his head forward. Usually I would close my eyes and experience—walls held little erotic interest for me—and I wondered if he was doing the same.

My fingers traveled down, sliding over the smooth skin and finally hitting the subtle bump of James's tailbone, then fanning out to coast along the round curve of his cheek and down to his thigh. As I turned my attention, and my touch, to the delicate warmth of his inner thigh, he abruptly let his head sink downward and he shifted his knees farther apart to allow me better access.

His cheeks were still clenched, but they parted at the simple urging of my hands, revealing the hidden hole behind, pink and tense and waiting. I slid a finger around the crinkle of skin surrounding it, leaned forward and let my breath hit that spot, inhaled the peculiar odor there.

James's thighs were trembling. Was he wondering what I was thinking? Was he afraid I was disgusted by the sight of him?

I wasn't. Though I let my hands drop from the split of his ass, I couldn't take my eyes off the curves on display for me, the picture he made sprawled there, waiting for my touch, my penetration. Heat pulsed in my belly and cunt. I wanted him.

I tore my eyes away from him long enough to locate the lube and pop it open, then squeezed some of the clear liquid out onto my fingers. It was cold and shiny and slick and did its best to dribble down my arm before I could get it to its intended location, but couldn't quite escape. I slid three wetted fingers across the tightly clenched muscle, feeling the slight give of it, and the more pronounced rejection.

Judging things adequately lubed for a more thorough exploration, I reached forward and touched James's neck, getting his attention. "You're okay with this?"

"Please," he said, his voice nearly breathless.

I didn't need more encouragement. I slid a finger to the hole, pushed, felt it resist then finally give my finger entrance to the deep warmth of his body. Even while I was adjusting to the sensations, while I was digesting the sudden rush of excitement that flooded my body as I made these realizations, he was pushing back on my finger, thrusting it deeper with an insistent push.

He froze, and I could hear his harsh panting even from my removed distance.

"I'm fine," I said, squeezing some more lube onto my finger and delving deeper.

"Me, too," he said, matching my movements.

I found myself rocking in unison. I slid a hand beneath him, past his balls, found his straining penis, slippery and throbbing, and closed my free hand around him. He pushed himself back, thrusting my finger so deep my knuckle was against his ass, and then shuddered and groaned and I felt semen jet from him.

He thrust again a few times, gently, my hand milking his cock and his asshole tight around my finger, then collapsed against the mattress. I slid my finger from his ass, pulled my hand from beneath him, and got up to wash.

When I came back to the bed he was lying on his back, smile on his face, eyes shut. Beside him lay the bottle of lube—a little had leaked out—and the unused plug. I hadn't even thought of using it once my finger had gotten involved. I'd wanted to explore on my own, not through a plastic substitute.

I gasped as my seemingly conquered lover suddenly sat up, wrapped himself around me and pulled me to the bed, where he promptly sank a suspiciously wet finger in my ass, and returned to his abandoned position of mouth-to-cunt until I was writhing with delicious pleasure, crying in unavoidable orgasmic release, and finally sighing in bone-deep lethargy.

It was James who picked up the plug and lube, after giving me a kiss on the forehead with lips smelling of my own juices. It was James who cleaned himself up, and cleaned me up, and pulled down the covers and tucked me in. It was James who clicked off the light before climbing into the bed beside me and pulling me into his arms.

I just had the presence of mind to say, "Next time it's my turn."

I don't know if James said anything to that, but the tight hug that pulled me to him spoke volumes, and I knew, even as the world slipped away, that I had a few adventures to look forward to.

A WINTER'S TAIL

Veronica Wilde

Vanessa lay naked on the bed with her legs spread wide, her creamy bottom turned up. Heavy velvet curtains were pulled against the falling snow outside, but that sensual languor of the winter afternoon swam through her blood, relaxing her and making her eager to start filming. Behind her, A.J. fussed with the camera. They'd made five videos so far and this was always the part that felt awkward to Vanessa—waiting for the camera to start running so she could slip into action. At least this time she was on her stomach, which felt natural. Sprawling on her back with lights trained between her legs made her feel like she was at the doctor's office.

She brought her long black hair over one shoulder and stretched, enjoying the softness of the velvety purple blanket against her nipples. They were borrowing their friend Skylar's apartment for this shoot because it was tricked out in a lush and gothic décor, from overstuffed sofas to dark and moody paintings. They didn't always go goth for their shoots, but they did try to find unusual and beautiful settings. That was the goal of their shoots—not to make money so much as create authentic, visually arresting porn.

Skylar walked over to the bed and looked at the toys waiting next to a bottle of lube: a lavender dildo, black anal beads of a soft, comfortable plastic, and a classic egg-shaped, silver bullet vibrator. "You've done this before this, right?"

"Five times," Vanessa said, then wondered if she was talking about making dirty movies or having toys in her ass.

"Almost there," A.J. grunted. "The lights…"

Vanessa didn't ask for clarification. A.J. tended to lapse into the elliptical when she was working, and after six years of friendship—the first two as lovers—Vanessa knew better than to disturb her focus.

A knock on the door did it instead. "Oh, there's Nate!" Skylar cried, and went to the door.

Vanessa looked over her shoulder in alarm at A.J., who frowned.

"Uh—no," A.J. said as Skylar led a tall, dark-haired guy into the bedroom. "I don't know who this is, but we don't do spectators."

"He's here for the shoot," Skylar said as if it were obvious. "You said Vanessa couldn't find the right guy—"

"Which is why we're doing toys!" A.J. said. "You can't just invite some stranger over and expect Vanessa to fuck him!"

"Uh…I'm not a stranger." Nate laughed awkwardly and waved at Vanessa.

Her pale cheeks flushed. If only he was a stranger. That she might be able to work with—showing off for him, letting her exhibitionist side rise as she showed him her pussy, then the pretty starfish of her asshole hidden between her famously voluptuous asscheeks. Maybe she'd even let him work one of the toys slowly inside her until she was moaning and begging him to go deeper.

Instead Skylar had brought over Nate, the cutest barista at her café. The same café where she worked on her poetry several nights a week. The café where she went tongue-tied whenever Nate drafted her latte or stamped her café punch card, because he was so sexy with his floppy black hair and amber, almond-shaped eyes that her normal flirting abilities froze around him.

"I don't get it," Skylar said. "You said she couldn't find the right guy."

Vanessa rolled over to face them, leaving her legs open to give Nate a clear look at her pussy. Sure enough, he blushed. "Here's the thing," she said. "I only let toys and fingers in my ass. And tongues. But actual penises? No."

"That's what I meant when I said she couldn't find the right guy," A.J. explained. "Vanessa is…picky."

Vanessa could see the confusion on Skylar's face. She clearly had assumed, as so many people did, that any woman willing to be filmed having sex, let alone posting it online for everyone to see, was up for any kind of sex, with anyone.

Skylar sulked. "So now what?"

A.J. looked at Vanessa. She shrugged. "He can watch." She tried to sound indifferent as she said this, as if it wouldn't affect her at all to have those sexy amber eyes watching her play with her ass. Then she realized no one had asked Nate what he wanted. "Uh—what were you expecting?"

He laughed, embarrassed. She realized this had to be awkward for him, too, showing up at an amateur porn shoot ready to fuck a woman he'd never met.

"Skylar just said you needed a guy on hand for one of your movies," he said, "and I, uh, volunteered."

One of *her* movies? That sounded like he'd seen them before. Like he'd known it would be her.

"So what won't you do?" A.J. asked practically. "Have you even been filmed before?"

He shook his head. "No, I haven't, but I'm willing to try anything."

Vanessa and A.J. glanced at each other. They'd had problems with guys before in their movie—guys who thought it would be the hottest thing ever to star in amateur porn, but then had trouble staying hard with a condom on, or got annoyed when A.J. directed them to change their position.

Vanessa shrugged. "Let's just start and see how it goes."

A.J. started filming. Vanessa slumped back on the pillows and spread her legs with a smile, caressing her nipples and giving the camera an unfettered look at her plump pussy lips. This was always a turn-on for her, showing off naked for the camera, knowing how her performance would electrify strangers. But having her secret barista crush watching made it feel more taboo, more shameless to dip her fingers into her pussy, then pull them out gleaming with transparent strands of wetness.

She sucked her fingers clean, loving the sweet taste of her own pussy. Pulling back her clitoral hood, she made her swollen pink bud pop out. If only she wasn't being filmed, then she could check Nate's facial expression, but instead she smiled at the camera and teased her clit with just a fingertip. She was so sensitive right now that just mild pressure would make her come. And that wouldn't do at all.

She rolled onto her stomach and slid her hand between her legs, fingering her cunt with her thighs wide open.

"Hot, very hot," A.J. said.

Vanessa turned her head to the side. Nate was still as a statue, eyes locked on her pussy. She pushed her fingers in deeper, rubbing herself in slow circles.

"I am so horny," she said in a shaky voice. "Can you help me?"

He was by the bed in a second, both eager and hesitant. Their gazes locked and she knew this was going to go somewhere extraordinary, on film at least.

"Get naked," she told him. "Take your dick out for me."

Nate pulled off his T-shirt and jeans, revealing a long, hard torso that seemed all muscle and tattoos. His thick cock slapped his stomach, as smooth and hard as she'd always fantasized.

He knelt on the bed and looked questioningly at the camera. "Don't look at me," A.J. said. "Look only at Vanessa."

A shiver of delight swept down her back as she felt Nate's knees nudge hers. "The lube and the silver bullet," she said, trying to keep her voice calm. "Let's start with that."

She played with her clit, praying she wouldn't come too soon as she felt the cool, slippery toy push against her anus. There was no telling how much experience Nate had with anal and if he knew to go slow and gentle at first. But the toy pushed a little farther, penetrating that initial resistance, and then slid into her cavity. The vibrations filled her ass, reverberating into her pussy, and she pressed harder on her clit, turning her pelvis into a buzzing, euphoric swirl of erotic energy.

"Oh god." She didn't want to come yet, not already. But something wet and soft washed over her cunt: Nate's tongue. His hot agile mouth nibbled her lips and teased her clit, making her gasp right before his tongue pushed into her slit. She groaned, long and deep. She'd never had a tongue in her cunt and a toy in her ass at the same time, and it drove her into a mindless, writhing sensation of pure ecstasy as she kicked and rocked on the bed.

"Oh god," she blurted and then she was coming all over the bed, pussy squeezing in rhythmic pleasure as Nate circled the toy in her ass.

She sprawled on the bed, thrilled and a little embarrassed. Her pussy was tingling and she was out of breath. Somehow it seemed impossible that the hottest barista in town had just eaten her out while fucking her ass with a vibrating toy.

"That looked good," A.J. said. "Really good. You two really work together visually."

Vanessa glanced over her shoulder. Nate was still waiting between her legs with a hard seven-inch cock, his damp dark hair rumpled. *So hot*, she thought dizzily.

"We're not done already, are we?" he asked. He sounded disappointed.

A.J. assessed his cock with a glance. "If you can keep going, so can we."

As they drank the bottled water Skylar handed them, Vanessa ran her eyes over Nate's tattoos. She wanted to suck him until he ejaculated in a flood down her throat, wanted to ride him until she came. But there was a camera rolling and she and A.J. had a specific agenda. This was to be the anal video—*A Winter's Tail*, they had titled it. And she didn't accept penises in her ass.

Nate's sexy amber eyes met hers as they drank. She gathered her courage and stroked his cock. "How do you want to come?"

Nate looked surprised, as if they were back at the café and not naked on a bed together. "Uh, whatever's in the script."

She put his hands on her breasts. "How about fucking my tits?"

His cock twitched and she smiled. She could see a thin strand of precome connecting his swollen crown to his flat stomach. "I...whatever you want."

She traced his fingertips around her nipples. "This isn't all about my ass, you know. I want you to have fun." She looked at A.J. "What do you think? Nate fucks my tits and I make him come, and then we get back to anal with the other toy?"

A.J. nodded. "Sounds good. You two have an intense energy. We should exploit it."

Vanessa lay back on a small ramp of pillows, Nate straddling her chest. She hadn't yet been tit-fucked on camera and she was curious how Nate's thick cock thrusting between her soft, round breasts would look. But the real show for her was Nate, his floppy dark hair tousled and his face flushed as he bit his lip, working in and out of her cleavage. He was going to come soon. Hungrily, Vanessa sucked his cock into her mouth, tonguing his sensitive head. "Oh *fuck*," he breathed, which she took as a signal to unleash her hands, tickling his balls and stroking his shaft as he jerked on top of her, emptying a salty-sweet load of come down her throat.

"Oh god," he groaned and fell back on the bed.

A.J. lifted her head from the camera. "I think you killed our stunt cock."

"Nice work," Skylar said. "I'm impressed."

Vanessa grinned, pleased with herself, and drank the rest of her water. She poured a few drops on Nate's stomach and he sat up. "I'm back," he said. "Back and ready for action." He looked at the pillow pile. "How about you lie over this? It'll give me better leverage and probably give her a better camera angle."

"He's right," A.J. said. "Get your hips right on top, Vanessa, and spread your legs as wide as you can."

Vanessa paused. She could already tell how crude it would look, her hips elevated and her pussy and ass split open for the taking, her face and upper body hidden behind the pillows. But that was point of their videos, wasn't it? To make hot, dirty little movies that were raw and partly unscripted.

Somewhat awkwardly, she draped herself over the pillows, sprawling down with her face in the bed. "I can't reach my clit," she began, but Nate took her hands and pushed them back on the bed.

"You don't need to," he said. "I'm in charge now."

A thrill of submission raced through her. A.J. was filming and she felt deliciously like an object, an anonymous set of legs, ass and pussy that had been provided for Nate's—and the audience's—enjoyment. And Nate seemed more in his element now, teasing her clit with his tongue and gently fingering her ass. She writhed, breathing faster. This wasn't about her posing or arching her back or tossing her long black hair around, all of her pretty video tricks. This was just her succumbing to the thrill of the talented fingers and tongue working her over.

A cool hardness prodded her pussy. Nate was sliding the lavender vibe into her, rubbing slowly in all the right places. She sighed with pleasure, then surprise, as the tip of the anal beads eased into her ass. Oh god, yes; he was double-penetrating her with two toys. This was what she lived for. He gently pushed the beads inside her tightness, making her squirm, then slowly withdrew them until she cried from sheer delight. He was hard again, his erection pressing into her leg, obviously as excited as she was. Then something hot and soft dipped between her cheeks—Nate's tongue tickling her ass.

His mouth moved on her like an expert's, awakening nerves she hadn't known she had. She clawed at the bed, groaning helplessly as the toy in her cunt and the tongue in her ass worked in tandem. Grabbing the blanket, she rocked herself back and forth on the pillows, rubbing her clit. Desire and need were rocketing through her body in a deep and primal demand. "Fuck me," she begged, half-senseless. "Please, Nate, fuck me for real."

His tongue paused. Her face burned with heat as she heard herself say, "Fuck my ass. Please. I want you to."

No one said a word. The room was so silent that she heard

it all with excruciating anticipation: the rip of the condom foil, the squirt of lube in his hands. And then, Nate's sharp intake of breath as he positioned his crown against her asshole. For a moment, she was sure that his dick was way too big to take inside her tender hole. Then he pushed in, just an inch, impossibly large and yet filling her with a delicious, commanding sensation. His cock worked in another inch and she felt her body relax, her ass adjusting to this new, masterful domination. His breathing was so fast and tight. Slowly, he withdrew. Vanessa moaned with disappointment but she heard the lube dispenser go again, and then his cock was back, cool and slippery and reasserting its entry.

"Oh god," Vanessa breathed as her ass accepted its first full penis. He was sliding all the way inside her now, still feeling impossibly large but exciting, too, his balls resting against her pussy. "Oh please, don't stop."

Her body was no longer under her control. She was just an animal, a flushed and shaking body craving this thrusting in her ass. The vibrator was still half-lodged in her pussy and she pushed down on the pillows, rubbing herself as Nate's cock teased and fucked her ass. Leaning over her, he grasped her breasts.

"Hips up, Nate," A.J. said. "Just like that, cock in ass. That's what I want to see."

Nate kissed her neck, groping her tits. "I can't hold off much longer."

"It's okay," she panted. Her body was burning up, a rocket of sweat and sensation and bliss. He pushed his cock in with a final groan and her pussy broke into throbs, a clenching, searing orgasm that shook her from her ass to her clit. He squeezed against her with a raw cry and she felt his own orgasm rupture inside her. Then he pulled out slowly, leaving her ass sore, tingling and happy.

"Fuck me, that was hot," A.J. said. "And we got it all on film."

Vanessa clutched a pillow to her chest, suddenly sleepy and a little embarrassed. They always took her farther than she meant to go, these videos. She always gave a little more than she intended to give, learning something new along the way. Nate curled up next to her and kissed her shoulder.

"Did that hurt a lot?" he asked.

She shook her head. "I'm a little sore, because you're bigger than any toy I've had. But it felt good."

Skylar opened the curtains. It was still snowing. "I'm, ah, going to get coffee," A.J. said, glancing at them. "Skylar, why don't you come with me?"

When the door shut behind them, Nate pulled her to him and kissed her. His body was still wet and hot against hers but she didn't mind. "Did you know it was me you were showing up for today?" she asked.

He nodded, kissing her neck. "But I didn't know...it would feel like this."

She burrowed into his arms and watched the snow fall past the window, thinking of all the unscripted surprises their second date might hold.

NO REST
FOR THE SICK

Medea Mor

T he alarm clock read *12:18* when Becky Gallagher woke up
and opened her eyes. She started for a moment, thinking
that she was going to be ridiculously late for work. Then she
remembered that it was Sunday, one of her days off, and that
she wouldn't have been in any condition to go to work anyway,
had it been a workday.

She'd been in bed for two solid days, struck by the flu that
was doing the rounds. The day before, she'd felt so miserable
that she'd left her bed just twice, to stagger to the toilet. She
hadn't even taken a shower, fearing that her legs would buckle
beneath her if she stood on them for too long. Nor had she
taken Patrick up on his offer of running a bath for her, despite
the fact that she loved a hot bath more than she loved kittens
and cupcakes. All she had wanted to do was huddle under the
blankets, buried like a mole but sick as a dog.

Today was a different proposition. No sooner had she opened
her eyes than she realized that the headache and nausea that

had plagued her for the last few days had lifted. She still had a blocked nose and sore throat, but she felt human again, sufficiently so to leave her bed, she thought.

She also felt dirty. She didn't need to run a finger over her skin to know that there was grime all over her body, layers of dried-up sweat that urgently needed removing. She'd run a fever, Patrick had informed her the night before, and on top of that it had been hot and humid. She had a vague recollection of beads of perspiration trickling down between her breasts and along her spine as she lay tossing and turning. No doubt her pajamas and sheets could do with a good wash. First of all, though, she was going to wash herself.

She turned around to face Patrick, her partner and master of three years, who was sitting on his side of the bed, his back against the velvet-covered headboard.

"Good morning," she croaked.

He looked up from the book he was reading, a big science-fiction novel in which he'd been engrossed for the last three evenings. "Good afternoon, I think you'll find. How are you today, pet?" His glance was inquisitive but, she couldn't help noticing, a little less concerned than it had been the day before. Clearly, then, the improvement in her health was showing in her face.

"A little better," she told him. "So much better, in fact, that I'm thinking of getting up and taking a shower."

"Please do." He went back to his book. "You're stinking up the place." He didn't meet her eyes, but the smile curving on his lips told her everything she needed to know.

With a grin, Becky sat up and stepped out of bed. She was feeling weak and a little light-headed, the result, she thought, of the fact that she hadn't eaten anything for the last two days. She suddenly felt a craving for food—salty, savory food. She could

murder some toast and eggs, possibly even a full Sunday breakfast. First, though, she'd have a wash.

As she stepped under the showerhead, she could feel her sick
body spring to life, awakened by the hot jets of water. She lath-
ered up, washed her long, brown hair and shaved, luxuriating in
the feeling of being clean and smooth for the first time in days.
The only thing that was missing, she reflected, was Patrick.
She was used to him joining her in the shower on weekends,
either to force her onto her knees and let her pleasure him while
water cascaded down on him, or to press her into the tiles and
fuck her ass with long, deep strokes. Personally, she preferred
playing in bed, but that didn't stop her from straining her ears
for signs of his arrival every time she took a shower, or from
fantasizing about all the things that he might do to her in their
warm, fogged-up bathroom. The way it usually played out in
her head was they explored each other's bodies with their hands
while they soaped up. Once they had rinsed off, they continued
exploring each other's bodies with their mouths while the water
fell on them with that spattering sound that defined shower sex
for her. Then he would proceed to take her in any of the three
holes that were his.

As so often before, her fantasy of being taken by Patrick
instilled in her an urge to be filled, to have something hard and
solid inside her, to remind her of Patrick's magnificent cock. So
she toweled off and, having grabbed the lube bottle that sat next
to the shampoo and conditioner, stepped out of the shower. She
filled the washbasin with hot water, then took her Njoy plug
from the vanity and placed it in the basin. As she let the stain-
less steel plug soak up the warmth of the water, she began to
lube up her rosebud, taking care to make sure that the gel was
properly distributed.

Oh, she liked her Njoy. Not only was it a gorgeous plug

to look at—a work of art rather than a toy, she often found herself thinking—but she also loved the feeling of its smooth steel on her skin. A curved rod with a seamless ball at the end, the toy had the perfect shape and finish to feel comfortable in her bottom. And just as importantly, it had weight. She'd never realized how important that was until she had first inserted the wondrous toy and had been blown away by its heaviness and solidity. She'd hardly used any other plugs since.

Once the plug felt warm to the touch, Becky took it out of the basin and dried it. She spurted some lube onto it, then bent forward over the vanity and forced herself to relax as she inserted the steel toy, exerting just enough pressure on it to begin stretching the taut little opening of her ass. Millimeter by millimeter, the sleek metal slid past her defenses. She felt it moving into her, inside her, claiming her most private place.

Feeling pleasantly full, she made her way back to the bedroom, naked as the day she was born. Patrick didn't look up from his book as she lay down next to him, facing him. However, his right hand—the hand with which he wasn't holding the book— soon began to wander. It snaked its way to her body, settling eventually on her right breast.

With startling efficiency, he began to caress her nipple, rolling it between his fingertips as if to examine its consistency. She sighed, relishing the feel of his skin on hers, the pressure of his fingers. It had been several days since she'd last felt it, which was unusual in their relationship.

He withdrew his hand to turn a page, then put it down on his thigh.

"Please don't stop," she said, hoping it didn't sound too much like a command.

He looked up. "Are you actually up for that?" he asked, his voice full of surprise.

In answer, she grasped his hand and put it between her thighs. When he withdrew it, it was slick with her juices, as she had known it would be. She never failed to get wet when she was wearing her Njoy, nor did the feel of his fingertips on her nipples ever fail to elicit a response from her.

"Well now, that's interesting." He smiled, suddenly more interested in her than in his book. "How the hell did that happen?"

She giggled. "I suspect it's something to do with the plug that's buried in my ass, Master."

"A plug, eh? I wasn't aware I'd given you permission to insert a plug."

Becky stared at him in disbelief, wondering what on earth he was up to now. She'd never needed permission before to insert a plug. It was understood between them that he liked her stretched and wide open for him, and so she was encouraged to wear plugs as often as possible, for as long as she could bear. He'd never chastised her for wearing one without asking, nor had he ever seemed likely to. But that was Patrick for you—consistent in all things that mattered, yet likely to change rules on a whim if he felt like it.

"Get your plugged ass over here and let me punish you for this infraction," he ordered, smiling mischievously at her.

She was half-horrified, half-excited at the thought. "Don't you think I'm a little too weak for that?"

He shook his head. "No, I don't. If you're well enough to insert a plug and get wet, you're well enough to get spanked, I think."

She couldn't argue with that. "You're a cruel man, Patrick Fletcher," she told him, shaking her head at him.

"You know it, sister. Now be a good pet and get your ass over here."

She complied, a little hesitantly, even though she was fairly certain he was going to administer a play spanking rather than a punishment spanking. As he put down his book and swung his legs over the edge of the bed, she sat down next to him and draped herself over his knees, all too aware of the handle of the plug that must surely be visible between her buttcheeks. It must be a decadent sight, she thought, her naked ass splayed for his enjoyment with a plug sticking out from it. But she didn't feel decadent as she dangled from her master's knees with her head forced down. She just felt helpless—helpless and completely at his mercy.

As was his wont, Patrick kept her waiting for a long time, teasing her bottom with tender caresses and gentle pseudo-slaps before tearing into her. The wait did little to steady Becky's nerves. As she tried to find a comfortable position on his thighs, unable to use her hands because he was holding them behind her back, she felt her insecurity mount, wondering if this might not be a little too much, too soon. However, she reminded herself to trust Patrick, who generally seemed to intuit how much she could handle better than she did. She didn't think he had ever overtaxed her, although he'd come close on a few occasions.

As he peppered her bottom with playful swats, she found herself warming to the treatment, both literally and figuratively. Even so, she yelped when his hand suddenly came down on her ass with full force, landing heavily on the fleshy part of her buttocks. Her flesh quivered under the strength of the strike. She imagined it rippling on impact, only to feel another rush of moisture flow into her pussy.

He followed quickly with two more hard slaps on her now-burning flesh. They reverberated through her body, hitting the plug in her ass before echoing off it again, making her squirm in his lap.

Her body was responding to the spanking in a big way. Not only was her bottom tingling, hot and sore, but her clit rubbed against Patrick's shorts every time he hit her, as did her nipples, which had sprung up again, begging for her master's attention. She tried to ignore them, focusing instead on the hand hitting her tender bottom, but it was no use. Her whole body was alive, burning with need.

Three more slaps to her right buttock followed, layered for maximum effect. Becky howled each time his hand met her flesh. She felt her muscles clamp down hard on the plug, making her even more aware of her own delicious fullness.

After six hard slaps, Patrick paused to admire his handiwork, purring appreciatively at the sight that greeted him. "So nice and rosy. You were a lovely shade of pink when you emerged from the shower, but now you're all pink and burgundy. It's a fetching combination."

I'll bet, Becky thought, a little skeptical. She was decidedly heavy-headed now, what with all the blood pooling in her brain. What was more, her right buttcheek was burning as if her fever hadn't receded at all, but was merely concentrated in this one small part of her body. It made it all very hard for her to think straight, but she did manage one well-defined thought: *Is he going to continue spanking me, or is this the extent of what I'm expected to endure today?*

As if he had read her mind, Patrick let go of her hands. He didn't stop tormenting her, though. He merely moved his attention to the inside of her ass, lovingly running a finger down her freshly showered crack until it met the handle of the plug. He began to circle the sensitive skin around the plug, over and over again, until every nerve in her bottom was sizzling and her whole being was focused on the circular movement that was hypnotizing her, driving her mad with anticipation.

She moaned as he gripped the plug and started wriggling it in her ass, slowly and tenderly, stroking the bruised flesh of her right buttcheek with his other hand as he did so. She pressed herself against him, seeking both to steady herself and to rub her clit against his thigh. She could feel the tension rising inside her, needing an outlet, a release.

"Please fuck me, Master." If she hadn't had a red face already, she would have blushed at the words, and at the breathlessness with which they were uttered.

He didn't answer straightaway. Instead, he kept circling her asshole with one hand and wriggling the plug with the other, driving her crazy with the regularity of his movements until she couldn't help herself any longer.

"Please, Master."

He chuckled. "Always begging," he said, clearly enjoying her desperation. "I don't know why your parents called you Becky, pet. They should have called you Beggy."

She smiled despite her discomfort. "Please, Master."

"Not today, pet. Not until you're up and running again."

She felt a brief stab of disappointment, but had to admit he was probably right. What with her light-headedness, she'd probably pass out the moment he started driving into her in earnest. However, that didn't alter the fact that she was half-crazy with lust and badly in need of a release.

"In that case, will you please help me come some other way?" It was a bold request, but she didn't think he'd deny her, not after the couple of days she'd had.

She should have known better. She should have known that Patrick delighted in subverting her expectations, in doing things his way, just to prove to her that he could.

"I'm afraid not, pet." The pressure on the plug increased. So did the maddening throb between her legs. "However, you're free to play with yourself if you wish." He withdrew his hands from her body, to indicate that her over-the-knee time was over and that she could get up if she wanted.

Becky clambered off him, feeling the blood rush down from her head as she rose, a little faster than sensible perhaps. As he swung his legs onto the bed again and leaned back against the headboard, she flopped down next to him, facing him. She could feel the plug inside her, reminding her of its presence.

Looking up at Patrick, who was obviously enjoying watching her succumb to her lust, she put her hand between her thighs, spreading the wetness she encountered to the outlying regions of her pussy. Her clit seemed to burn under the pressure of her fingers, tingling much like her bruised bottom.

The sight of her touching herself seemed to spur Patrick on. He leaned forward and grasped a handful of one of her tits, with a firmness just short of painful. The touch sent a shiver of pleasure to her pussy, making her work her fingers just a little faster.

His thumb teased across her hardened nipple. Then, suddenly, he pulled at it, gently at first but then harder. She gasped, which elicited a chuckle from him. He pulled again, ostensibly to see if he could make her gasp again, then twisted her nipple as if he was trying to rip it from her chest. Fire shot from her breasts to her aching pussy, making her pussy clench.

She rolled onto her back, both to give Patrick better access to her breasts and to increase the pressure on the plug in her ass. Her burning backside throbbed as it met the mattress. She felt as if all her erogenous zones were pulsing at once, ratcheting up the ache of her arousal tenfold.

She needed a release, and she needed it soon.

"May I come please, Master?"

Again, he took his time answering her, or maybe it just

seemed that way because she was so on edge. Her arousal was so intense now that it bordered on painful. All her attention was focused on the fingers twisting her nipple and the pulse beating insistently in her pussy and ass.

At last he replied. "You may. And you'd better make it a good orgasm, pet, because it's the only one you're going to get this weekend." As if to emphasize his words, he twisted her nipple one more time, then pinched it tightly.

Her body couldn't take any more stimulation. As her fingers strummed at her clit, fast and furiously, release surged up to her head and down to her toes, making her clench her muscles around the plug in her ass. The ensuing contractions were so intense that they sent her into thrashing ecstasy. She surrendered to the pain and delight, relieved finally to be able to let go of the tension that had been building inside her for so long. Wetness soaked her hands as her orgasm shook her, running through her like a current of electricity.

He let her rest for a while as she lay next to him, curled up into a ball and breathless. Inching closer to him, she nestled her cheek against the soft cotton of his shorts. She thought she could feel his heartbeat beneath the fabric, but soon realized it was her own, pounding in her ears like a drum, racing with adrenaline and relief.

She wasn't given much time to recover. Just when she was feeling completely safe and relaxed, Patrick asserted his dominance over her again.

"Time to get up, pet. Time to go to the kitchen and make us some brunch."

She looked up at him, shocked and a little indignant. "But I'm sick!" she protested. "I can't be expected to cook when I'm sick, can I?"

He was firm. "I've looked after you for the last two days.

Now it's your turn to look after me. If you're well enough to come like that, you're well enough to cook us some brunch, I think." He picked up his book and started reading again, but not before shooting her his most wicked grin.

She rolled her eyes then got up, a little shaky but otherwise fine.

She supposed she did owe him something.

VIN ROUGE POUR TROIS

Erobintica

I dressed for undressing. Tonight had been on my mind all day. All week. Hell, all month. Ever since Jared had whispered his little "Would you like…?" in my ear during one rather exuberant session, I'd been anticipating this. When I'd said "Yes," his eyes had narrowed and he'd kissed me hard. Of course, I'd already been fantasizing along these lines, ever since he'd mentioned that he'd tried it once before. Well, almost. It hadn't worked out as he'd planned. There *is* that danger when you attempt to turn fantasy into reality.

Rummaging through my closet, I chose a pair of slightly older jeans. Tight, a little faded, but not ratty. We were starting the evening at a little wine bar and I wanted to look casual, but not too casual. Then I chose the brown and beige wrap top with a small design that camouflaged its see-through fabric. I fished around on the floor of the closet for my brown platform shoes, the ones with the ankle straps. Then I went to my dresser.

My dark brown lacy bra was right on top, an omen. It would

show through just enough. I could've picked the matching panties, but I wanted to offer a little surprise. So I chose my new cream-colored cheeky with the little lace-up in the back—a special pair for a special evening. I opted to go without jewelry. No need for anything small that might get lost during the proceedings. I dressed, sipping a black raspberry cabernet aperitif I'd made myself a couple of days before. Its dark, passionate color as I swirled it in my glass made me tingle. Just the thing to get my blood warmed up. After brushing my hair and touching up the little bit of makeup I was wearing, I was ready.

I drove to Jared's place. He had a cute little bungalow near the restored downtown area. We were going to walk to the wine bar, only a few blocks away. I smiled to myself, already feeling aroused as I parked in front and saw him waiting on the porch. His face was serious as I walked up the path and climbed the stairs.

"You sure you want to do this?"

I laughed. "You think I would be here if I didn't?"

His smile competed with the lustful look in his eyes. He slid an arm around my waist and pulled me into a kiss. His hand gave my ass a little squeeze. We stood there, tongues reassuring each other that this was something we both wanted. I couldn't resist and lifted my knee and pressed it against his crotch.

"Okay, Tory, we'd better head over there now. We don't want to be late."

Jared took my arm and led me down the steps. As we walked past all the nicely restored houses from the twenties and thirties, we engaged in small talk: what work had been like this week; that his neighbors, the ones with the barky dog, were gone for the weekend; how he'd arranged everything, gotten his place prepared for later. My mind kept wandering. I'd always had these leanings, these wants. But until I'd met Jared, I'd never admitted them to anyone. Would it be like I'd imagined? Soon we were downtown.

Turning in at an iron gate, we crossed a brick courtyard, passing under the curved branches of a gorgeous old live oak. There, waiting at the entrance to the wine bar, was Doug, the man Jared had been telling me about on our way here. They'd met last winter while working on a project in the valley. There hadn't been much to do in the evenings, so they'd hung out at the hotel bar and split pitchers of beer. Things get said under those circumstances that might not otherwise. Turned out they had some interests in common.

"Hey, Doug! This is Tory. Tory, this is Doug."

Doug was gorgeous. Not that Jared wasn't, but for some reason I hadn't expected his friend to be this Norse god type. Jared was lovely in his own way—slim, with dark hair and a subtle goatee. Sexy in a geeky way. I was hoping that Doug found me at least slightly attractive. Oh, Jared had assured me he would, but every now and then I worry, since I'm not your leggy blonde bombshell.

"Delighted to meet you, Tory. Jared's told me so much about you."

Was that a twinkle in his eye? What had Jared told him? I laughed, relaxing already. We passed through the heavy timber door into the bar. The place had a cave-like quality, with real stone walls and flickering sconces along the walls. The tables were set in cozy little niches, intimate and good for quiet conversation, among other things. Jared and I came here often. We were shown to our little round table and ordered a bottle of pinot noir right away, while we perused the sharing menu. A very good-looking guitarist played on the small raised stage at the end of the room. Yes, I was always looking.

We ordered the stuffed mushrooms and baked brie with

berries and chatted about your typical getting-to-know-someone topics—movies, jobs. The waiter brought the wine and performed the whole wine snob ritual for us. When he finally left, we raised our glasses and Jared gave the toast:

"To a night we've each separately dreamt about and together will always remember."

We clinked.

I felt flushed and squirmy already and I hadn't even taken my first sip. Raising the glass to my lips, I glanced first at Jared, then Doug. They were both watching me. I took a long sip then licked my lips as I put my glass down. At first there was an awkward silence at the table. What to talk about in this situation?

"This guitarist is great. He plays here regularly, has his own style. Very sexy."

Did I say that? Sexy? Well, the guitarist *is* sexy. Those intricately tattooed arms. The dark eyes. Those hands. I like watching him play. But tonight he might not get as much of my attention.

The food arrived. We ate and drank, and soon a second bottle was ordered. Our tongues loosened by the pinot—once referred to as "sex in a glass"—we soon were exchanging one double entendre after another. Legs and knees bumped. Hands brushed arms. I was definitely feeling the wine. Warm and wet. I rubbed my ankle up Jared's shin, watched him smile and felt his hand on my thigh, lightly stroking. Doug said something funny and I laughed, reaching over and placing my hand on his shoulder, letting it linger.

Jared leaned in close, his voice just above a whisper.

"Go ahead. Touch her. Under the table."

Doug deftly slid his hand under the tablecloth, edged closer to me. Then I felt his fingers brush the side of my leg, right at the seam of my jeans. It was like an electric shock. Jared's hand was still on my other thigh, running up and down the inside of my leg, yet never getting too close to the trembling, damp center of my consciousness. Then Doug's hand moved up and over the rise, settling directly over where my clit sat thrumming, seemingly in time to the guitar that was at the edge of my awareness.

What I was very aware of was that their hands had met under the table, on me, and in concert had started kneading, pressing, making me delirious. I couldn't take much more of this.

"Oh my god, I think it's time we got out of here."

I finished my wine and set down my glass.

"Come on, guys. I don't want to embarrass myself here."

We paid and left a generous tip since our waiter had been very discreet, not constantly bothering us. Doug excused himself to use the restroom, and Jared and I headed outside to wait for him. We stood close in the filtered light under the oak. Shadows played across our bodies as the slight breeze, somewhat cool, caressed the branches. I pressed myself to Jared and our lips met in a pinot noir–soaked kiss.

"Thank you for this."

"Not much has happened yet, Tory."

"It's already wonderful."

"It's still early. Just wait."

We heard the door and Doug emerged, walking across the bricks to join us. I smiled and took his hand and we started walking. Doug's hand was so large and warm. Jared placed an arm around my shoulders. We didn't pass anyone, but I wondered what they would have thought of our trio if someone had. We reached a corner and stopped. Jared took me in his arms and gave me a deep, slow kiss. He then let go and I turned to Doug, who slid his hands around my waist. I kissed him.

Their mouths were so different, yet both warm and welcoming. I shivered. Sighed. Then we all laughed.

"Let's get the hell back to my house, I'm about to bust through my pants."

"Well, mine are soaking wet already."

Doug reached toward me.

"Shall we check? Sure enough, she's sopping wet."

Yup, we were no longer at all self-conscious and I was so anxious to get to Jared's and get out of my clothes that I grabbed both their hands and pulled them across the street. We practically ran the last half block. Jared gave my ass a little slap as he moved toward his door. I laughed and gave Doug's cute buttcheek a squeeze. He reached over and found my nipple, ready and quite vigilant, and gave it a quick twist. I cried out in delight just as Jared turned the key in the lock.

Inside, we found the living room set up with the night's planned activities in mind. Jared had prepared the fireplace, and soon flames lit the room. Plenty of pillows, candles arranged to provide just enough light to see from all angles. On the coffee table there were another bottle of wine, three glasses and a pump bottle of lube with a small bowl of condoms. He'd thought of everything.

While he poured wine that probably wasn't needed, I went to take my shoes off and Doug helped, stroking my feet and sucking on my toes. Jared bent, lifted my hair and kissed the back of my neck. I closed my eyes and let the bliss take me, losing track of whose hands were where. My wrap top was unwrapped and pulled from my shoulders. Hands caressed my breasts, slid inside the lacy cups of my bra. A hand undid my jeans and crept between my legs, where my pussy was soaking wet.

I opened my eyes and saw Doug. He pulled me to standing then slid my jeans down. I stepped out of them as Jared gave a little whistle.

"Like them panties. Look, Doug."

He spun me around and kissed me hard as Doug ran his hands over my ass. It felt like every inch of my being was sparking and they were still clothed!

"No fair. I want to see *your* bodies. I'm gonna take turns undressing you guys one item of clothing at a time." I smiled. I don't think I'd ever been so hot.

First came the shirts. First Doug, then Jared. My hungry tongue kissed their necks and chests then flicked their nipples. Next my hands moved to belt buckles, zippers. All the while their hands wandered over me, slipping a bra strap down, teasing my legs open, caressing my throat. My pussy was so swollen and wet that I was sure I would come with the slightest touch. With their pants gone, I reveled in the sight of their cocks. Jared's I knew—it was long and slim. Doug's was thick though, and I immediately knelt and took it in my mouth.

He let out an "Ohhh," while Jared said, "Wow, this is so hot."

I sucked at Doug's cock for a while, then turned and took Jared into my now puffy lips. His hands strayed through my hair, then grabbed and pulled me away, turning me back to Doug so he could unclasp my bra. I stood and Doug bent to take a nipple in his mouth, kissing and tonguing it while I leaned back, and Jared kissed my mouth while pressing his hard cock against the lace barely covering my ass. His hands reached around and slid into my panties, into the flood that was my cunt. Just then Doug gave my nipple a little bite and I came, shaking and clinging to his shoulders.

There would be no rest for the wicked, though. Jared slowly removed the last shred of clothing, my little lace-up undies, and tossed them to Doug, who gave them a sniff and sucked on them. I was seriously on the verge of a swoon worthy of any

Victorian lady—I wondered how many had experienced this sort of exploit.

There was surprisingly little talking going on. Jared was usually noisy—that's how I'd learned he had the same fantasy as me. But now we were all sighs, grunts and growls. We'd made it to the floor. Doug had buried his face in my pussy and his tongue was coaxing me toward another orgasm. How many would I have tonight? Jared kneeled over my face and I hungrily devoured his cock again. Just then Doug pulled away from me, and I felt the rush of cool air on my drenched flesh. He was reclining, watching us, his cock a flagpole. Jared reached down, slipped his fingers into my cunt. I almost came again.

"I think she's ready for you, Doug."

Oh, was I ever ready. I straddled him and slowly lowered myself. His exquisite girth took my breath away. We started moving together, and I felt Jared behind me, kissing all along my back from my neck to the dimple that rose and fell with my ass. I couldn't believe I was still so turned on. I'd usually be coming down now. I fucked Doug, excited because I knew Jared was watching. I'd been afraid that I'd be seized by an unexpected shyness. That I'd shut down sexually because of some unknown fear when it came time to make this a reality. But it was real.

In the huskiest voice I'd ever heard from him, Jared said, "I think it's time you got fucked like you've always wanted."

My brain was about to explode. I heard the wrapper tearing open. Heard the pump of lube being depressed. Felt Jared's hand press me forward onto Doug's chest, then his fingers basting my twitching anus, sinking first one, then another, and then a third finger into my ass. I groaned.

I heard his voice whisper in my ear, his breath reaching into the deep, red desire blurring my mind.

"You ready for this?"

"Oh god. Yes."

He removed his fingers one at a time. Doug stopped pumping, pulled out a bit and lay still. I could feel the warmth radiating from Jared's body as he moved in close. I felt him press his cock slowly into me, stopping momentarily when I moaned, then continuing when I mumbled, "More."

With Jared deep inside my ass and Doug pressed into my cunt, I found myself growling as we all started to move. At one point, I think I sunk my teeth into Doug's shoulder, but he didn't complain. When I came, it wasn't just an orgasm. With both men racing toward their own climaxes, it was ecstasy, rapture.

And the night was still young.

THE SUPPORT GROUP

Fiona Curtis

T he man at the front of the room shifted awkwardly from one foot to the other and cleared his throat before he spoke.

"My name's Eddie and I'm an alcoholic."

"Hi Eddie." The group issued its standard response.

As the group's newest member began his tale, Sally sighed and glanced at the clock on the far wall. Another twenty-five minutes to go.

"It's not that I want to get back on the crazy train," she explained, as she grimaced at the taste of the lukewarm coffee. "I don't want to go back to drinking again. Well, obviously I do or I wouldn't be coming to these meetings. It's just that..."

She slumped into the cracked faux-leather seat and fiddled with a paper napkin.

"Just?"

"Just...I don't know if I can do it with these damn meetings. They're so...so boring. There—I've said it. Week after week of self-pitying droning. I know I have a drinking problem but god do we all have to be so frickin' miserable all the time?"

Across the table, Sally's sponsor Dan chuckled. She was sure he'd heard all this before. Or maybe he hadn't. He was about her age and she seemed to remember him saying he hadn't been a sponsor for very long.

"And don't tell me to give it time or to try another meeting." She continued her rant as she ripped apart a third packet of sweetener and poured it into the cup. "I've tried meetings all over town and they're all the same. 'My name's Mookie and I'm an alcoholic.' If part of being sober is to never be cheerful again, I may just die of boredom."

Other than that brief chuckle, Dan had been sitting patiently, waiting for Sally to finish. He pushed a piece of piecrust around his plate with a fork. Sally looked at him expectantly.

"Any words of wisdom, boss?"

"You want me to tell you to go have a drink?"

"Of course not. But hell, there's got to be something better than this. I can't even get laid because it's against the rules—"

"You know you shouldn't swap—"

"...Dependency on the bottle for dependency in a relationship. I know." Sally had heard it over and over again, but it offered little consolation at the moment. "I'm a nun. A sober frikkin' nun. Just give me a robe and I'll spend the rest of my days in silent devotion. Sister Sally...with nothing to live for. Well, maybe nothing but a vibrator and butt plug hidden under my habit." She smirked.

Dan said nothing but looked at her thoughtfully. He checked his watch, pulled a ten-dollar bill from his pocket to cover his coffee and pie and got up to leave.

"Gotta go," he said. "Just promise me you won't go and do anything you might regret."

Sally grinned.

"Don't worry, Dan. All my daiquiris are virgins from now on. Unfortunately, so am I."

The following day, Sally finished her shift at the bookstore and arrived home to find a voice mail from Dan.

"Listen, Sal, I've been thinking about what you were saying. There's another meeting I go to. Just a private group, but I think you'd be a good fit and might find it helpful. Not as stuffy as the regular times. Give me a call if you want to come along."

After calling her sponsor back, Sally learned that the group would be meeting in a few days' time. Dan didn't say much but assured her everyone in the group had the same goal—to learn to stay off the drink while venting their frustrations and having a good time. He arranged to meet her at the diner so he could drive them both there.

In the car, Sally was sure Dan seemed rather evasive. He gave only the vaguest of answers to her questions about the group, but at the same time he seemed almost excited. The meeting turned out to be in the large living room of someone's home. Comfy sofas and floor cushions surrounded an odd little glass coffee table. Sally was somewhat surprised to find that, including her and Dan, the group consisted of just six people: three men and three women. Dan made the introductions and they welcomed her warmly, agreeing with Dan's assessment that she would be an excellent addition.

"You see, Sally," a slender blonde named Katherine explained when they were all comfortably situated, "we are all recovering alcoholics. But we know that regular meetings can be a little dull, to say the least." She smiled knowingly at those in the room. "And we all have needs." Her voice took on a breathy tone as she said "needs." Looking directly at Sally, she continued. "So tell me—is it a big butt plug?"

"Wh...what?" Sally gulped uncomfortably, but she noticed that Katherine leaned closer, revealing a delicious view of her full, unfettered breasts beneath her silk blouse.

To Sally's right, Joe spoke up as his hand carelessly caressed Jill's thigh.

"It's okay. Dan told us all about your toys. You're in safe hands here. Let's just say we all like toys, and we've found a safe way to ease everyone's...frustrations." He nodded at Dan. "I'd say it's time."

Sally's sponsor stood, and she couldn't help but notice the erection straining against the zipper of his pants. He reached toward Sally.

"We all take turns...you know, to avoid any dependency. And I promise you, I'll be better than any butt plug."

He pulled Sally to standing position in the middle of the room and began to unbutton his shirt. Katherine and Jill had started undressing each other and fondling their breasts. Joe unzipped his pants and was now stroking his rather large penis.

Nervousness and excitement overwhelmed her. Without the slightest hesitation, she stripped off her top and skirt and stood facing the group in her underwear. Scott unhooked her bra, allowing her breasts to fall exposed. He then slid her panties down to her ankles.

"You won't be needing these," he whispered.

"Just a few rules," Dan said. By now, he too was naked and his erect penis bobbed to and fro, a hint of moisture glistening on its tip. "No one else is to know. And as your sponsor, I get to take you first. And everyone gets to watch."

With that, he led Sally toward to the small glass table and motioned for her to kneel over it. The table was empty except for a bowl filled with what looked like brightly colored candy. Looking closer, she noticed that the candy was in fact condoms and lube in a variety of flavors. Mesmerized by the position in which she found herself, Sally took a glance around at the others. On the sofa to one side of her, Joe was sucking one of Katherine's breasts while Jill had started to masturbate. All of them continued to eagerly watch her.

Reaching from behind, Dan began to caress her left breast, his right hand trailing down her belly to find her wet pussy. And wet it already was. But instead of stopping there, he allowed his fingers to continue, trailing her moistness all the way to her other entrance. Without a word, he rubbed her juices around her hole and slowly eased a finger in.

"You were right about that butt plug, baby. You won't need much warming up at all." Waving one of the brightly colored packets before her face, he asked, "Cherry? After all, it does seem appropriate."

Jill was now sitting on Scott's lap and appeared to be grinding onto his erection, still rubbing her clit and staring at the show in the center of the room.

Dan inserted a second finger into Sally's asshole, ensuring that she would be able to take his girth. She felt him spread the lube in and around her hole. When he decided she was ready, he gently inserted his shaft. Having seen him naked earlier, she wondered if she could take it all. With a gasp, her question was answered, as he pushed his entire length into her. His cock filled her better than any toy ever could.

Sally groaned as she found her rhythm, pushing and pumping in time with Dan, who clutched her hips and built up speed as he withdrew almost completely before once more thrusting as deeply as he could. Eventually he hit his pace and began to ram for all he was worth. Balls slapped and breasts swayed in time with the thrusts. Sally couldn't remember a time when she had felt so deliciously full. She frantically gasped and squeezed tighter around Dan's cock, enjoying the sensation of complete anal impalement.

Katherine crawled toward her and, without breaking Dan's rhythm, took one of Sally's nipples in her mouth. She sucked and flicked it with her tongue while Joe fucked her from behind. The room was a mass of flesh and juices. Jill bounced energetically on top of Scott, still fingering her sopping clit. Scott grunted beneath her, commanding her to squeal for him.

Dan moved faster still, so fast that Sally wondered if she could keep up. Knowing that they were both close to the edge, Sally reached for her clit and frantically strummed away, bringing herself to the brink of orgasm. As she felt the first waves of ecstasy wash over her, Dan clutched tighter, and with one deep thrust, he emptied himself into her. Katherine bit one of Sally's nipples, causing her to cry out from the added intensity. Across the room, Jill also screamed a frenzied climax.

A river of come dribbled from Sally's ass as Dan pulled out and turned her to face him. At once, Katherine's tongue took his cock's place, greedily licking the salty juices. From his vantage point, Joe had been able to watch the show while still fucking Katherine. As he reached his own climax, he signaled to Jill to come and clean him up, an offer she readily accepted.

Soon, everyone lay piled in a naked, sweaty, come-covered heap. Hands carelessly fondled whatever breast or cock was nearby, as they gathered themselves for another round. It was Sally's sponsor who finally spoke.

"Sally," said Dan. "On behalf of everyone here, I'd like to welcome you to A.A. *Anal Anonymous.*"

LIGHTS OUT

Angela R. Sargenti

The lights flickered and died, along with the TV.

"Some drunk probably hit a pole again," said Brian. "Now what are we going to do?"

I knew I had to think fast or he'd break out the cards or Monopoly, both of which I hate.

"Don't worry," I told him. "I'll think of something."

So I went into the bedroom, lit a bunch of candles and looked around. Brian has this stiff backrest pillow he uses when he reads in bed, and as soon as my eyes lit on it, I thought of a different use for it.

I flung it facedown in the middle of the bed and stripped my clothes off before buckling the harness around my waist.

Just the feel of all that cool leather surrounding me made me horny. I pinched my nipples hard and a bolt of desire shot through me.

"Yoo-hoo. Brian. Come here."

He poked his head into the room and said, "The strap-on?"

"Yes. Here. Bend over this." I gestured to the pillow. He got naked in a hurry and climbed up and over. The backrest put him at the perfect pitch and angle for a rear assault. I sank to my knees behind him.

He smelled clean and slightly yeasty and I began by massaging his ass, balls and taint.

I felt his breathing change as he became aroused. Sinking down farther on my knees, I spread his cheeks for a go at his puckered little hole.

Brian gasped when he felt my tongue connect and I teased it around and around, circling his tasty little bud like he circles my clit when he's eating me out. I let my tongue skim his taint as far as it would reach, then it was right back up to that perfectly tight and delectable hole.

His balls felt snug in their sac and I liked the weight of them, the way they felt in my hand. I fondled them a bit and he shivered in delight, spreading his knees farther apart as I tongued him fiercely and aggressively.

He pushed back with his hips, but I wasn't done with him yet.

Not by half.

I slid a finger into my pussy and moistened it, and then I teased *that* around, too.

"That's my pussy juice, Brian. My pussy juice is going in your ass tonight."

He moaned, appropriately turned on, so I fingered myself again, and this time I slid it straight up his ass.

He tensed for a moment, then he relaxed as I pumped my finger in and out a few times before slowly, *slowly* withdrawing it.

Brian groaned in frustration.

Good, I thought.

I'd have him begging by the end of this, begging for that long, thick dildo to be buried up to the hilt before the night's end.

With that goal in mind, I crawled off the bed and smacked his ass and thighs a few times.

"There," I told him. "You stay right there and let that warm up a little."

I slipped off to the kitchen to get the glass dildo from the freezer and some other things from the fridge and pantry.

When I returned, he was waiting there, hyperalert, every nerve alive and ready for me to spring my next move.

Well, let me tell you, I didn't disappoint.

I shook the can of whipped cream I'd brought back and squirted it all over his scorchingly hot asscheeks. He flinched a little when the cold hit him, and I chuckled.

"Yummy."

I shook some candy sprinkles into my hand and scattered them liberally, and finally I sank a cherry in on top, wedging it right between his cheeks where the cleft of his ass began.

"Perfect," I told him. "A butt sundae."

I leaned in and trailed a finger down his crack, scooping up some of the sweet cream in the process.

"Here," I told him, offering up my finger. "Taste."

He sucked eagerly and grabbed my hand for more, but I was on a mission to tease, so I pulled away and bent down for a taste of my own, lapping up huge, wide swipes with my flattened tongue, carefully avoiding all contact with his sensitive areas.

When he realized this, he clicked his tongue impatiently.

"Always in a hurry, aren't you?" I asked him.

And he said, "I need you."

"And you shall have me. Later. When we switch places."

Without another word, I reached down under him. His dick

was hard as a rock and I stroked it, and then I bent down to finish cleaning him off.

When I stood up again, I reached for the pizza peel, and I drew back and gave him a good whack on the ass.

He tensed, but held his position, so I gave him a few more before tossing it aside and kneeling down between his legs once more.

I grabbed a bottle of lube off the nightstand and dribbled it straight down his crack.

He groaned again, the warmth and cold too much.

"Poor baby," I told him, rolling the side of the cool glass dildo over his hot, aching butt. He sighed in relief and probably thought I was ready to mount him now, but he was destined for disappointment.

Instead, I greased the tip of the dildo with some lube and thumbed his asshole as I coaxed it in.

Brian caught his breath sharply.

"Oh, baby, please."

"This is nothing," I told him. "This is nothing compared to what you're going to get."

He moaned again and I pumped the smooth glass in and out, just gently and leisurely enough to drive him mad.

"I'm going to fuck this ass tonight, fuck it good."

I popped the dildo out and flung it aside, picking up the thick wooden peel again and spanking him relentlessly. He surrendered to it, sprawled over the pillow helplessly, grunting with each hard blow.

"I'm going to ream you out like you've never seen," I told him, reinserting the glass dildo. "I'm going to fuck you with my big, huge dick."

"Please," he told me. "Please."

"Talking back?" I demanded. "Well, you'll have to be

spanked for that impertinence."

By then Brian was at his wit's end to have me fuck him, but I pushed him a little more by dropping the paddle and teasing him some more. I traced little patterns on his reddened ass and pinched the sore spots on his bottom.

Finally, I rose to my knees and lubed up my fake penis.

It looked real enough, though, veins sticking out and a nice big tip on the end, and when I finally entered him he almost wept with relief.

"I'm fucking you, Brian. I'm fucking you with my pussy juice and my big dick. You like that, don't you?"

He hissed out a yes, and I bumped him hard all of a sudden.

"You're my bitch, aren't you?" I asked him.

"Yes."

"Then say it. Say, 'I'm your bitch, Sabrina.'"

"I'm your bitch, Sabrina."

"Tell me how I should punish you later."

"With my belt."

"That's right. With your belt, your own belt, the one you wear every day to work, so when you're there on Monday you can think about this all day long while you're sitting on those welts."

"Yes, Ma'am."

I fucked him harder, hard enough to grind his cock against the pillow. With every push, I got a faint whiff of the sawdust that pillow was stuffed with, and Brian grunted with each shove. When I felt he was close enough to coming, I grabbed hold of his hips and made him stop.

"Oh, please, Sabrina!"

"No. Not yet. Not yet."

I ran my hands up and down his back, palms flat one time,

nails out the next, scratching and petting and driving him insane. And he longed to rub one out against the velveteen cover of the backrest, but I loved this far too much to see it end.

Reaching beneath him, I grabbed his dick and jacked it a couple of times, and then I let go and went back to screwing him.

"You'd better hold out as long as you can," I told him, "because as soon as you come, you're going to be whipped hard. You understand that, don't you?"

"Yes, Ma'am."

"Good. Good boy. I just might have to reward you later."

"Oh, yes, Ma'am. I'd like that."

I started up again at a dawdling pace, but this time he didn't complain or try to rush me along, although the threat of being whipped made him hornier than ever. He let me roll my hips and slap forward with my big, giant dick and hold him there, even though I knew he needed to be pumped instead of just pinned in place.

"I love you, Brian. You're being a very good boy right now and holding off like I told you to."

"Yes, Ma'am, but it's hard."

"I know it is, but don't worry. I'll take good care of you."

Well, I'm a girl who likes to keep her promises, so I started in on him again, fucking him slow and steady until I felt him straining so hard I knew he wanted to cry, and all at once I picked up the pace, ramming that dildo straight into his tight little ass and fucking him for all it was worth.

Suddenly he threw his head back and howled.

"Oh god, Sabrina, I'm going to come."

So I shoved it all the way in, like *I* had some jizz to pump out, too, instead of just him, and I felt him jerking around beneath me as he fucked the pillow as hard as he could until he was wrung dry.

"Jesus Christ, Sabrina," he sobbed, going limp, and when he was absolutely done, I pulled out.

"Oh, Brian, you're so fucking sexy I can hardly stand it," I told him, collapsing against him.

My own breath escaped me as I wrapped my arms around him from behind and lay my head against his sweaty back. We lay there drawing breath together as we recovered, and then I felt him stirring beneath me.

"Get ready," I told him, coming back to life myself. I went over to pick his pants up off the floor and pull the belt loose, and I doubled it over and snapped it so he knew what was coming next.

"I'm going to wear you out," I told him, "And then it's your turn to top me. And you'd better do a good job or you'll find yourself right back here beneath me, is that clear?"

And he said, "Yes, Ma'am. Oh yes, Ma'am!"

And lucky for us, the lights never did come back on until morning.

BAR NONE

Mina Murray

They weren't from here, I could tell. It wasn't that they looked provincial; it was more just that there was something foreign about them, even though they'd been at the bar regularly for the last few weeks and spoke excellent, unaccented English. Tonight they occupied the VIP booth they always reserved, discreetly tucked away into a dimly lit corner at the back.

I'd been watching them all evening. It was hard not to. They were seriously hot for each other, kissing and laughing softly and touching every chance they got. He wasn't what I'd call handsome, but there was something arresting about him all the same, especially when his hand slipped under the table to move between his wife's legs. I could feel the pulse between my own begin to thrum in response. When his eyes locked with mine, the beat intensified.

He beckoned me over, and I walked slower than usual, taking the time to smooth my expression blank. I was about to ask him for his order, when he gestured to his companion.

"Oh, it's my wife's turn to choose."

He turned to face her. I couldn't help but notice only one of his hands rested on the table.

"Mila, what should we have?"

His wife was gorgeous, with pale skin and waves of shimmering black hair swept over one shoulder to bare a long and elegant neck.

"I'm not s-sure," she stammered. "You pick."

"I couldn't possibly decide," he demurred, "not with such a selection. And what if there are specials?"

I took my cue, rattling off the name of every cocktail I could think of, complicit in their little game and enjoying every moment of it. I was halfway through my list when Mila came in a series of shuddering breaths.

"Martinis," she gasped at last. She looked up at me from beneath her long black lashes and smiled weakly. "Please."

When I came back with the drinks, they were gone. But they'd left enough to cover their bill, along with a generous tip, and a note that I pocketed to read in private. It was only toward the end of my shift that I could duck away, and by then the suspense was killing me.

My fingertips drifted gently over the buff-colored, monogrammed paper, tracing the variations in texture as if reading Braille. There was a certain ritual to handwritten communication that I missed. I read the words slowly. *We're heading back to Prague next week, but until then the city is our playground. We'd love for you to join us. Alec*

The offer wasn't unexpected. I'd been propositioned by couples before, but there was too much potential for complication. This was the first time I felt able to accept. I glanced at my watch. Not too late to call the number he'd given. When Alec answered on the third ring and I told him who I was, his voice warmed with pleasure. After agreeing to meet at the serviced apartment where they were staying, I raced home to shower and change, and to let my flatmate know where I was going.

It was a long trip up in the elevator. I checked out my reflection in the gilt-edged mirror along the back wall. I looked nervous. I was starting to have second thoughts when the elevator stopped and the doors opened onto the penthouse. I took a couple of tentative steps before Alec came into the hall and greeted me with a kiss on each cheek. I inhaled the scent of his cologne, a spicy and masculine scent of bergamot, pepper and tobacco that warmed my blood. He ushered me inside and called out to his wife.

"*Miláčku*, Katherine is here."

Mila had been lounging on the huge bed in the center of the room, draped in a silk kimono so beautiful it made me feel underdressed. I had been expecting the same continental welcome I'd received from Alec, but when Mila rose to greet me, she kissed me full on the mouth. It was a gentle kiss, her lips brushing softly over mine, though it soon became demanding. I wasn't sure if she had deepened the kiss, or if it was me; all I knew was that her tongue was in my mouth and my hands were in her hair and her breasts were pressed up against mine and I was moaning.

"How rude," Alec said, interrupting our kiss. "I should have offered to take your coat."

Mila laughed and stepped back so he could help me out of my jacket. When he pressed a burning kiss to the nape of my neck, the roughness of his beard abraded my skin and I shivered, nipples beading tightly beneath my flimsy camisole.

We sat down on the couch by the window and Alec handed me a glass of champagne. I was grateful for the prop. I suddenly felt shy. It might have been the way they were both looking at me, with such open appreciation. Or maybe it was just that I wasn't sure of the protocols for sleeping with a couple.

"We're so glad you called," Mila said.

"Well, I'd seen you at the bar a few times, and you—"

"Put on a good show?"

"Mila likes an audience," Alec said, "and so do I. Especially one as sexy as you."

"So do you two play in public a lot?"

"No, not all the time," Mila answered, "mostly just when we're on holiday, away from home."

"I haven't really done this before," I confessed.

"What?" Alec asked. "A ménage?"

"A married couple."

"Don't worry," Mila purred, "we're good at sharing."

The cushion dipped as Alec shifted his weight, moving closer so he could gently bite the back of my neck and skim his hands down my arms so delicately that the fine hairs there stood on end. And then he took his hands away, and in one swift motion pulled the straps of my camisole down over my shoulders, baring my breasts and trapping my arms at my sides.

Mila darted forward and took one of my nipples between her teeth, rolling it against her tongue. I gasped and arched off the couch, my head tilting back until I could see the naked heat in Alec's gray eyes as he moved to claim my mouth. My lips parted for him immediately. I'd always loved being kissed upside down; the sensations felt so different it was as if we had invented an entirely new act. His hands went to my breasts, to cup them and lift them and pluck at one peak while his wife teased the other. I cried out into his open mouth and felt a shudder run through his frame.

Alec broke the kiss and had started to unbuckle his belt when Mila sat up and I felt a cold rush of air on my breast's wet tip.

"Alec, *moje láska*," she chided, "you promised I could have her first."

Alec looked anything but contrite. He had clearly been about to release what looked like a very impressive member from the confines of his jeans. My lips tingled at the thought. I shrugged free of my cami to grasp for him, but Mila sucked my fingers into her crimson-painted mouth and my eyes fluttered closed.

"If you're that responsive now," Alec laughed, "I'm really going to enjoy watching you with her mouth between your legs."

My sex clenched at the thought. Her tongue was doing magical things to me and I could guess what it would be like for her to do that...elsewhere. She bit the sensitive pad of my fingertip one last time, then got to her feet, utterly self-possessed, which didn't seem fair while I was naked from the waist up and coming apart at the seams, cheeks flushed and panting.

"Alec," she ordered, "help Kat undress."

There was a gleam in Mila's eyes that had me a little worried and more than a little excited. The meek creature I had met at the bar was fast transforming into some glorious predatory animal, all sleek flanks and lethal intent.

The room was silent, except for my short breaths and the metallic sound of Alec unzipping my boots. He let me step out of them, then unbuttoned my jeans and dragged them off me, along with my panties.

Mila stalked forward—there was no other word for that fluid, rolling walk of hers—backing me up against the foot of the bed. I knew I had to find my voice or she would eat me alive. Call it the law of the jungle.

"How come I'm naked, and you're not?" I challenged.

She smiled, then unwrapped the kimono and let it flutter to the floor. She was breathtaking—from those long legs to the shiny black triangle of pubic hair between them to the long strand of pearls that circled around and under her breasts. I was surprised to see one of her nipples was pierced. I reached up and flicked it. She shot me one hard look, just one, and I gave it up to her straight away. She pushed me onto my back, and then her mouth was on me, and a slim finger crooked inside me, and I thought I'd come then and there. But I didn't. Mila stilled until my breathing slowed and the flush I felt all over my chest had faded away. Then she started licking me all over again.

She took her time, kissing my cunt like she was making out with it, all lips and tongue and nipping teeth. I heard a shuffling noise, and turned my head to find Alec standing beside the bed, entirely naked. The shadow cast by his erection looked like a long blade against his torso, with the point ending just beneath his heart. I wanted him to straddle my chest, to feed his cock into my mouth, to see if he tasted as good as he looked, but Mila had already started stroking him. Her movements were choppy and slightly awkward, not that Alec seemed to mind. He was thrusting into her fist as if it was her sex, but it was me he was watching. I could feel his gaze on me like a physical touch, and boy did it burn.

"Mila, stop, she's about to come."

"I'm not," I protested, "please, I'm not."

But we all knew I was lying.

"Is this how you treat all your guests?"

"Only the ones we like," Alec said, clambering onto the bed and maneuvering me on top of him.

Mila's arms snaked around my waist, holding me still when all I wanted to do was *move*. I almost screamed in frustration. When she used her whole body weight to push me down onto her husband's waiting cock without preparation or ceremony, though…well, then I screamed for real. My body was ready for him, theoretically. Mila had seen to that. But it was still a shock. The way he hit my depths would have been painful if I hadn't been so aroused that I felt like I could fuck the world.

Alec gave me a moment to adjust to his thickness, his length, then shifted experimentally, testing my resistance. He withdrew completely and I whimpered.

"Shh, easy," he murmured, and entered me again, but slowly this time, inch by heated inch, his progress smooth and inexorable.

Mila kept her arms around me as Alec started to stir. She rubbed her breasts against my back, braced her legs beside mine, and rocked me into each of his thrusts, mewling as if he was fucking us both. There was something so lewd about the way they were using me—as if I was just a beautiful, live toy—that turned my desire white-hot. I wound my arm around her neck and took her mouth, my tongue tangling with hers.

When Mila released her hold on me, I started writhing, and she reached down to feel where Alec and I were joined. With my legs spread, it was an easy thing for her to work some of our combined slickness between my buttocks. She positioned the back of her hand between our bodies so that the joints of her fingers pressed against my asshole, and their tips pressed into her sex. Every time I moved my hips, I forced Mila's fingers against us both. She moaned in my ear and Alec echoed the sound when my pussy clutched at him tighter. He grabbed my hips, and the cold band of his wedding ring dug into my skin. That little detail, that reminder of how I was caught between them in more ways than one, set off sensations that sparked like fireworks all through my body.

Alec had kept his steady gaze on me the whole time I came, but now he looked past me, to his wife. I felt a sudden stab of jealousy at the way he stared at her, so hungry for her, so greedy, even though it was me he was buried inside. He nodded slightly, and it must have been some predetermined signal because Mila gently pushed me forward so I fell onto him, against the hard planes of his muscled chest. I didn't know how I felt about them having choreographed our lovemaking in advance. But I knew how my body felt about it. I swiveled my hips, grinding my clit against the base of Alec's cock. I bowed forward to bite his lower lip, and I don't think he was expecting teeth, because he gave a little jerk and cried out. But he recovered quickly. Where his wife's kiss was sensual, Alec's was fierce and desperate, like I was some enemy he wanted to subdue. His hands wound into my hair and tightened, and he growled low in his throat as I gushed over his cock.

Something liquid hit my lower back, cold at first, but warming on impact. It smelled like cinnamon. Mila's hands caressed my back, ghosted down my spine, over the small of my back and down the cleft of my ass. My heart started racing as she knelt behind me to lick at my rosebud with her soft wet tongue, soon replacing her tongue with her probing fingers, slick with lube. The alternating sensations had me so crazed with lust that I felt no discomfort at all when she slid her finger into my ass, right up to the hilt. Alec twisted out of our kiss to look over at our reflection in the mirrored wardrobe beside the bed. When he saw Mila bent over me like that, his cock leapt and stiffened inside me and I knew that I wanted him to take my ass, too.

I was incoherent, inarticulate with want. But Mila knew what I needed, and dripped more lube onto me. When she thrust two fingers into my ass, the liquid heat flared again and then I started to beg.

"Please, Mila, please!"

"Okay, dear one, okay," she said, and helped Alec slide out of me. I could feel him start to shake as she gripped him, adjusted the angle of his cock, and slowly lowered me onto him.

I'd thought he was a tight fit in my pussy, but that was nothing compared to the way he filled my ass. Even prepped as I was, I had to employ every breathing technique I knew to avoid clenching up. Once the head of his penis was past the first ring of muscle, though, it was much easier, and then he was sheathed in me completely, and *fuck* it was good. He wriggled his hand between our bodies and pressed a finger inside my sex, curling it to hit my G-spot, and then I was the one fucking him, holding his shoulders down as I impaled myself on him, again and again and again.

When Mila got up off the bed, a spear of panic shot through me, and I reached blindly for her hand. I couldn't bear for her to leave, not now: I needed her with me till the end of this. But she just pressed a kiss to my shoulder and said, "Don't worry, I'm only moving in front."

Alec looked at me, his eyes dark with desire, as his wife lowered herself over his mouth and blocked his view. His long tongue snaked out and started circling her clit before she'd even had a chance to settle into position. Her hips undulated, her movements sinuous as she rode him, her breath coming in quick little gasps that matched my own. If Alec's tongue was as skillful as the fingers he had curled inside me, Mila would soon break. I was surprised Alec had been able to hold back for so long. His self-restraint was definitely fraying, though, and he bucked up into me, no longer content to let me control the pace. The unpredictability of his rhythm, the look of bliss on Mila's face, the way Alec's palm was rubbing my clit were all too much. I felt like my entire being was broken open, and I fell forward against Mila, sobbing and cursing as I came.

"Fuck, oh fuck, oh fuck."

The dam had burst, and Alec came, too, so violently that

I could feel the waves of his seed jetting into me. My tongue joined his on Mila now, and together we licked and sucked and bit until the waves of pleasure crested and broke over her and she cried just as we had.

Later, when we had showered and changed and I had conceded I was going to stay the night, I felt something rolling around underneath my pillow.

"Whose is this?" I asked sleepily, holding up an elaborately decorated glass dildo, with a base designed to fit into a harness.

"That's yours," Mila said, eyes sparkling with mischief. "It's for round two. And you get to put it wherever you want."

SEAT BELTS

Kate Dominic

My husband and I take lots of cross-country trips in our twelve-passenger van. Terry's a freelance photographer. I'm an independent web accountant. When he gets an assignment, we put the luggage rack on top of the van, fill it with our camping gear and hit the road. Due to the modifications he's made, we privately refer to the van as our personal bordello: two Scotchgarded captain's chairs up front, a small kitchenette and living/play area where the middle seats used to be, and a bench seat in the back that runs the full width of the van and opens up into a very comfortable bed, one now complete with four-point restraints.

For the past week, I'd been spending even more time in back than usual. The tinted windows kept prying eyes from seeing anything inside but the captain's chairs up front. The thick, waterproofed mattress was covered with thousand-count Egyptian cotton sheets. Pillows were piled around me so I was comfortable no matter which way I was situated.

Not that Terry placed me in restraints while we were moving. He was a tyrant about me being upright in my chair then, with the standard lap and shoulder harnesses securely fastened. Normally, we made a point of minimizing distractions for whichever of us was behind the wheel. But this week, Terry was doing all the driving. He told me to make all the noise I wanted, so long as it was "the background music" of me whimpering and pleading in my pretty black leather harness with a thick-necked anal dilator stretching my sphincters as we bumped along the rural highways and back roads he'd chosen to get us to Bismarck.

Terry had become a tyrant about a lot of things this past week. Before then, I'd never have imagined him giving me orders, much less my obeying them. Yet all it had taken was a few short days, and my pussy creamed at the sound of his voice telling me what to do. Every time he said, "I'm going to fuck your ass when we get to Bismarck," little pre-climax tremors ran through my body.

Terry's dick was average length, but it was really wide. I knew it would fit. He'd finger-fucked me to screaming orgasms, four long, strong, wide fingers buried up my bottom all the way to the knuckle, more times than I could count. But every time I saw his stiff, fat shaft with its huge bulbous head, my anus panicked. No matter how long and tenderly Terry fingered my anus or teased it open with his tongue, the minute he rose up over me or even the few times he tried pulling me over him, my sphincter tightened like a vise and it stayed that way. I wanted him in my ass. He wanted to be there. But my body just would not cooperate.

Last Sunday night, after another failed attempt that ended up with us both so frustrated and sore we just masturbated next to each other, Terry held me until he thought I'd gone to sleep.

Then he got his phone off the nightstand and went online. The next day, when a delivery truck dropped off memory cards and a new lens for his next assignment, there was a package for me as well.

When I reached for the package, Terry took it. My jaw dropped when he opened it, first because he'd done so without asking me, then when he pulled out a black plastic case marked Anal Dilators. Before I could begin to figure out what to say, he put the case on the sofa and took me in his arms. He held me close and rested his chin on my head, his hands warm and firm on my bottom.

"We can teach your body how to do this, Christa. But I'm pretty sure the only way it's going to work is if you let me be totally in charge. You need to learn to trust me not to hurt you, even when you're lost in pleasure." His erection drilled into my belly. "Oh, babe, I'm going to bring you so much pleasure." His hands kneaded my bottom as he spoke, his fingers warm and strong, sending delicious frissons of heat up and down my crack and over my anus as he rubbed my asscheeks together.

"The new assignment is in Bismarck. It'll take us the rest of the week to get there in the van. Will you do things my way that long? Let me be totally in charge? If I can't make you come by then, just by fucking your ass, we'll try something else."

He kissed me with lots of tongue, his hands still moving. God, I wanted him fucking my ass. When I came up for air long enough to say, "Yes," he hauled me to the couch, stripped me naked and shoved his pants to his knees. He knelt and pulled my hips to the edge of the cushions, and he fucked my pussy slowly, kneading my ass the whole time, until I screamed and we lay shaking and spent against each other. When he'd caught his breath, he pulled up his pants, moved onto the couch and took me on his lap. We took the shrink-wrap off the black plastic case together.

It felt weird sitting there naked, with him fully dressed, but when I reached for my clothes, he just said, "No." I was hyperaware of the feel of his jeans beneath my bare behind. He stroked the side of my hip and toyed with my bottom as we looked at the series of anal dilators—silicone butt "arrows" in gradually increasing sizes. The "arrowheads" were smooth and rounded, the blunt tips pointed just enough it was clear they could nose their way through the most tightly clenched pucker. Each head flared gradually, but a lot, ready to stretch even the most reluctant anus over the ever-increasing diameter. When the arrowhead had finally popped inside, the back edge tapered off quickly, forming a barrier preventing the head from popping back out, even as the sphincters continued their slow, slick glide down the rest of the smooth, straight and very wide shaft. A large disk at the base kept the dilator from slipping all the way in, even when the person was too lost in sensation to keep track of where the end was.

Terry explained this to me in graphic detail, sliding each dilator through my hands, smallest to largest, until my pussy creamed in anticipation. I don't know why they weren't scary, while his cock was. The heads were huge. Even the shaft of the largest was so big, my mouth went dry just looking at it. I rubbed my finger down the long, sleek length.

"Two inches in diameter," Terry nodded. "Almost as wide as my cock. When your bottom can comfortably take this, it'll be ready for fucking."

My sphincters clenched at the words, but if he felt my buttcheeks moving, he didn't let on. And he didn't stop talking. The dilators weren't the only things in the package. Terry showed me the black leather harness they fit in, pointing out the details in the workmanship as well as the specifics of how the harness would hold the dilator securely in my ass—no matter what! His gruff, clipped voice let me know he was dead serious about us doing this. He showed me where a dildo for my pussy would go as well, if and when he decided I'd earned a reward. There was even a pouch for a clitoral vibrator for when Terry wanted me to practice coming with my anus dilated almost wide enough to take his cock. Not all the way wide enough. He promised the first thing opening me that far was going to be his cock moving up my ass.

God, his talk and his bossiness turned me on. The smell of the leather and his shower soap, and the feel of his fingers stroking my juicing pussy, had me so turned on again, my whole body felt hot. But when I reached to unbutton his shirt, he pushed my hand away, and once again said, "No."

"We're training your bottom, Christa, starting now, while you're feeling all loose and relaxed from coming. We're going to start out with the littlest dilator and move up from there."

And right there in the living room, without even taking his shoes off, he bent me over with my hands on the sofa cushions and my legs spread wide. He took out a bottle of thick, squishy gel and worked his well-lubed finger into my bottom— one finger, two, then three, until I was slick and slippery and panting and so horny, I didn't care anymore that I was naked and he wasn't, or that he was giving me orders. All I cared about was coming.

Then he touched the tip of the dilator to my anus.

As always, my sphincters closed and locked tight. I lowered my head, sighing in total, tense frustration.

"I hate this," I muttered.

"It's okay, sweetie." Terry stroked my lower back and my bottom. His hands felt so good, caressing the hypersensitive skin where my bottom met the tops of my thighs. "Just pay attention to my fingers and concentrate on breathing. In. Out. That's it.

Deep and slow. Hold your mouth wide open and feel the air sliding in and out. Over your tongue. Down your throat."

He didn't say the R word. Every time I'd ever tried to make myself "relax," I tightened up more. He didn't push the dilator into me. He just held the smooth, cool, slippery tip against my anus with a firm, steady pressure that gradually had my sphincters opening around it. Sliding over it. The farther the tip slid in, the wider my anus stretched. Nothing hurt. It just felt so weird. It felt good!

I gasped as the back edge popped through. The rest of the shaft was noticeably thinner than the edge had been, but it was still wide enough for me to feel the stretch. Now nothing was impeding the long slow, delicious glide in of the cool, thick rod.

"Oh, WOW!" My lips curved up, my pussy quivering in sympathy. I took another deep breath and looked back over my shoulder. Terry was grinning.

"You like?"

"Uh-huh! UNH!" My smile faded as the friction passed. My anus clamped down hard on the dilator. Now that hurt! But unlike Terry's finger, the silicone shaft didn't give. It stayed hard and stiff—and wide, holding my anus open regardless of how much I squeezed.

Ooh, I squeezed! I couldn't help it! I closed my eyes, clenching my ass muscles as hard as I could! I gripped the cushions, mashing my lips together and holding my breath as sweat popped out along my shoulders.

"Open your mouth and breathe. Now!"

I gasped at the snap in his voice, instinctively doing what he said.

"That's it. In and out. Now open your hands." Terry was tapping the base of the dilator. "If you really want me to take it out, Christa, you know I will."

I couldn't keep squeezing while he was tapping. I told myself I knew the moment I said, "Out," the stupid damn dilator would be eased from my bottom, and kept out until I said it could go back in.

Then I realized my sphincters weren't hurting so much anymore. In fact, the more I thought about it, the tapping was keeping me very aware of how sensitive my anus was. As Terry removed his hand, the feel of my anal lips kissing frantically over the shaft was making my bottom and my pussy and pretty much that whole area feel really, really good. I took another deep breath and decided I was okay with the way the dilator was doing its job.

"It can stay," I smiled wanly. "It's just kind of weird." This time when I squeezed, my pussy quivered in sympathy. That absolutely did not feel bad! My face heated as I shyly ducked my head.

Terry laughed and buckled the harness around me. He slowly stood me up, laughing even harder as I moaned. I wasn't really uncomfortable. It just felt so odd standing up with something filling my bottom and keeping it open. I automatically kept my legs apart, gradually relaxing enough for him to take the dilator out, put it into the harness and slide the slicked-up shaft back in. Terry buckled the harness in place. Then he got a sundress from the bedroom and pulled it over my head. The friction over my bare nipples made me shiver. I squeezed the dilator even harder. I barely noticed when he slipped sandals on my feet. I was trying not to strain, trying not to bear down to force the dilator out of my bottom. My body was bearing down on its own, though, fighting the elegantly sturdy harness that was holding my anal stretcher firmly in place. The friction back and forth had pussy juice and lube running down my thigh.

Terry put the box of dilators and the dildo in his backpack

with a huge bottle of lube. Then he took my hand and led me out to the van. I'd never imagined what it would feel like to walk with an anal dilator filling my bottom. My hips swayed with each step, creating just enough friction to keep my attention completely on my anus—and the object in it. I threw my head back, breathing hard as I squeezed my sphincters tighter.

"You are so incredibly sexy," Terry laughed. He stroked gently over the back of my hand. "Your head's held high. Your shoulders are back. Your nipples are poking out like I've been sucking them for hours." His hand moved to my hip. "Your tummy's pulled in. Your bottom's squeezed tight." He cupped it and squeezed. "With every step, your hips roll in this sexy, swaying gait that makes my dick throb to fuck you." He leaned over and kissed me. His tongue swept into my mouth. I stuttered to a stop.

"I'm not going to fuck you, though." His breath was hot on my lips. "I'm not going to fuck you again until you can take my dick up your ass. You're going to do it in Bismarck, Christa. We're leaving now. The van's already packed. You can email your clients from the road. Tell them a personal situation has come up, because baby, our reclaiming our sex life is the biggest priority of our lives."

He swatted me. I jumped—and clenched the dilator. My moan came from somewhere really deep inside me. Terry just laughed, and patted my bottom again.

"Keep walking. I want to be on the other side of town before traffic gets bad."

Terry had to help me with my seat belt. I was so stunned at the sensations radiating from my bottom that I couldn't speak. My entire body was awash in hot flushes of new and different pleasures combined with the deliciously dirty knowledge I was out in public wearing only a harness and an anal dilator beneath my dress. My pussy was juicing so much the seat was wet beneath me.

I was also totally off balance realizing that for the first time ever, I was letting someone else take control of my body. It was shockingly sexy.

"Damn, Christa, you're gorgeous." He set my purse and the backpack that held my laptop, tablet, phone and files in a cubby in back of us. Just as he'd said, everything else from our suitcases to the cooler and a case of water bottles was already in the van. Then he climbed into the driver's seat and started the engine.

The vibration shot straight up my ass and through my pussy. I threw my head back, wailing softly as I climaxed, my pussy squirting onto the seat. Terry reached over and cupped my breast, stroking the stiffly pointed tip as I shuddered through one of the most intense orgasms of my life. The *click, click, click* of the ceiling camera barely registered as I arched into his hand and bucked against the soaking upholstery.

When I finally stopped shaking, I fell back into the seat, my breath still ragged as I slowly opened my eyes. Terry's grin filled his face, his gaze locked on mine as he fondled my nipple with one hand and clicked the camera remote with the other.

"You're going to get used to coming with your bottom stuffed, sweetheart. Because when we get to Bismarck, when I finally fuck you up the ass, you're going to come so hard you can't stop screaming."

His voice was rough and he was breathing hard. And god, his hands were shaking! But he didn't miss a beat.

"Get used to being naked, baby. I brought you just enough clothes to be decent when we go out—skirts and dresses only, no pants or underwear. Thigh-high stockings and garter belts. Your good black dress, because we are going to at least one five-star restaurant. Sexy bras, sandals, and fuck-me heels—and the pearls I got you for your birthday. I can't wait to see you in firelight wearing just pearls, stockings, and your harness and dilator. Your ass is going to be stretched wide enough for me to fuck it by then."

The look in his eyes was totally predatory. He rolled my nipple between his fingers, smiling as another orgasm shuddered through me.

"Good thing this van has tinted windows, love, because you're going to be spending a lot of time skewered on your dilators, and even more tied naked to the bed with me fingering and tonguing your ass. I'm going to take pictures of every step of your training." He turned around and took off the parking brake. His eyes met mine in the rearview mirror. "And Christa, the night I think you're ready to take my cock up your ass, we'll go dancing—someplace where nobody knows us, but we'll always remember, because you're going to do it with a dilator stretching you."

Oh, god, I was going to come again!

"Can I f-finger my clit?" I stopped with my skirt halfway up, not really sure why I was asking.

Terry's eyes glittered, his lips curving as he once more set the brake and took my breast in his hand. I frantically rubbed my clit, climaxing while he rubbed my nipple, climaxing again as he moved away and put the van in gear. Then we headed out into traffic. Terry hit every bump along the way. I came more times than I could count, every time with my anus clenching frantically over the dilator filling my ass.

Terry got progressively bossier as we drove. The sound of his voice vibrated all the way down to my pussy.

"When we get home, we'll figure out how to do things from now on. I still want us listening to each other, working together as a team and being partners. But on this particular trip, unless you specifically say no—and I mean say the words, Christa, 'no, Terry, I don't want you being in charge anymore,' I'm going to be the boss. You're going to get so used to the sound of my voice telling you what to do, so used to 'obeying' me, that your body will automatically do what I tell it to."

Without taking his eyes off the road, he cupped my breast and thumbed my nipple. My pussy trembled as my anus squeezed the toy.

"When I say 'I'm going to fuck your ass,' your body is going to open for me. It's going to know I'll make you come so many times you'll be hoarse from screaming."

I groaned and clenched my sphincters. My pussy squirted onto the seat.

In reality, most of the trip was pretty normal. Most of the time, I wasn't wearing the harness. We did a lot of sightseeing, and I got some work done for a client who was being audited. But between being naked under my dresses, completely naked the rest of the time when I was in the back of the van, my time on the dilators and Terry's persistent fingering, I was constantly aware of my anus, and so turned on it seemed like my pussy was always wet.

Four times a day, we pulled into a rest stop, and Terry sent me in to pee. And when I came back, he took me straight to the back of the van, locked the door and stripped me naked. Then he laid me down on the bed with my hips on a pillow and told me to spread my legs and pull my knees up and back.

"I'm going to finger your anus now, Christa. Then I'm going to slide the smallest dilator in." And he proceeded to do exactly that. The first few times, the little dilator was the only one I could take. When it was finally in, I sat in my captain's chair for one solid hour, by the clock, trembling in my leather harness as my pussy creamed and my sphincters worked themselves into exhaustion over the smooth, slick, unyielding shaft. My clit was so tender I needed lube there as well to keep from getting sore while I masturbated and the van bumped over mile after mile of country roads and construction. Being stretched over the smallest dilator was only the first step. It wasn't long before my sphincters were loose enough that the head popped right back out as soon as Terry unbuckled the harness.

We celebrated by sixty-nining, his cock sliding down my throat till he came while he sucked my wildly throbbing clit through three orgasms that made the whole van shake. And while I was still panting, he braced his arms against the backs of my thighs and slid the second dilator in. I was so relaxed, it went all the way in the first time. Then once again, I lay there quaking and gasping as my sphincters rebelled. As soon as my breathing slowed, Terry pulled me to my feet, tugged my dress back over my head and led me back to my captain's chair. Moments later, we were back on the road, my fingers moving frantically over my clit as my sphincters clenched and shuddered over the smooth, hard shaft stretching them even farther open.

On the morning of the third day, I was ready for the third dilator. Terry told me I was doing so well that from now on, I didn't get to touch my clit anymore. From now on, I only got to come from anal stimulation, and only when he said I could.

I lay whimpering on the bed as he unbuckled the harness. When I had taken the first and second dilators easily that morning, he'd rewarded me with a dildo in my pussy, too. The climax from double penetration and rubbing my now almost raw clit was so overpowering, it had me almost seeing stars. When he unbuckled the harness and the dildo slid free, my pussy was so juicy and aroused, I almost came again. Only the pressure of his hand against my pubes and his stern, quiet, "No," held me back.

He took his time, slowly pulling the dilator free. The silicone was warm from my body, the heated friction leaving me shaking as he pulled the long, smooth shaft slowly through my sphincters and free. Cool lube touched my anus, then his fingers were in me, lots of fingers, stretching and filling me as I moaned and shook beneath him. Then the cool nose of the third dilator kissed my anal lips. Terry rocked the huge silicone plug, stimulating my anus, holding the dilator firmly against me, murmuring encouragement as I panted and shook. My sphincters stretched and burned, slowly opening around the noticeably wider shaft. Eventually, I couldn't help bearing down, pulling it in.

"Ooh!" The slick, smooth toy stretched me, wider and wider. Oh god, it felt good! It was going to make me come!

"Stop."

"Ooh, ooh, OOH!" The sudden pressure of Terry's hand stilling, of it holding the head partway in and partway out, had me panting and shaking. The stretch was almost too wide. I gasped, and as my sphincters relaxed, Terry pressed on the plug again. Then he started rocking it.

"I want to come." My legs and ass and pussy quivered as the sensation started building all over again.

"No," he said, and held the dilator still. If he hadn't, I would have come from the sound of his voice alone. When I finally stopped shaking, he rocked the plug again.

"You're going to come in Bismarck."

He pressed and rocked and teased until once more, my asshole kissed its way over the head of a bigger dilator, and I was once again quivering in my chair, my pussy creaming at the stretch and vibration of the stiff, thick shaft stretching my ass as the countryside blurred by outside.

The next day, I took the fourth dilator. I had to work up through the first three every time. And for ten minutes out of each harness time, he made me get out and walk with the dilator in. It wasn't until he played back a video of me walking along the edge of a wheat field that I realized how much my hips swayed now with every step. Every movement felt like sex to me, taboo, dirty, ass-fucking sex, and I was doing it in public, even though nobody but Terry and I knew it. I was doing it because Terry told me to, and because following his orders made my pussy juicy and my nipples stiff. My asshole clenched and stretched and worked its way over the smooth, solid, slick shaft, my sphincter nerves quivering with every step. Obeying Terry kept me so desperately horny all I could think about was getting his cock in me. Getting it in my mouth and my pussy, and more than anything, into my ass.

By the morning of the fifth day, my ass was finally so loose, Terry could pull the next-to-biggest plug out without my having to strain. I had gapes now. Terry showed me video on the laptop, giving a running play-by-play as he fingered my now embarrassingly, deliciously wide-stretched anus.

He stuffed lube into me, massaging my gaping anal lips, the friction making me pant and tremble and *crave* until I was so eager to be penetrated, I moaned in pleasure when the slick, firm nose of the biggest plug started slipping steadily in.

"Please," I whimpered, "Oh, please, Sir!" The dilator was huge. My sphincters were stretching, more noticeably than they had even the very first time, burning almost to the point of pain, except this time, my whole body reached hungrily for the sensation.

"Breathe," he ordered, teasing the head in and out, pressing it deeper each time I inhaled. He rocked it back and forth, stretching me, opening me, making my asshole tremble and burn, making it so hungry I could feel lube and pussy juice running out of me. For the first time, it was truly almost too much. I almost told him to stop. Almost. I bore down hard, gasping as the head unexpectedly popped in. In one long, smooth glide, the entire shaft slid in deep. My sphincters snugged up tightly around it, clenching and squeezing.

"It burns!" I panted. "It's too big!"

"It's not as big as my dick," he snapped. Just like that, I relaxed, letting the spasms take me, sobbing as I shuddered and leaned into his hands.

"Oh, Sir."

His hands were so big and warm, his voice so low and comforting—and so implacable.

"Take it, Christa," he said, holding his hand steady on the base of the shaft. He looked deep into my eyes, letting me see into his as he slowly, gently, and with exquisite tenderness rocked the dilator in me. "Open your mouth wide and breathe. Feel the air going in and out, just the way my cock is going to. Take it like you're going to take my cock. Tonight. We're almost to Bismarck."

By now, every time he said the word, my pussy hummed. It took a long while, but eventually, I took the biggest dilator. When I could finally stand, I was stretched so wide I walked bowlegged to my seat. I shuddered as I put my weight on the cushion, letting the friction of my sphincters working themselves over the huge, unyielding shaft roll over me, stimulating my pussy and my ass—letting myself sink into feeling open and vulnerable, into the sound of Terry's voice, the sight of his erection tenting his jeans, and later that afternoon, the sight of the low city skyline.

We were in Bismarck, where Terry was going to fuck my ass.

He rented us an exclusive hotel room, taking my hand and leading me casually through the lobby with both the biggest dilator in my ass and a dildo the size of Terry's cock in my pussy. But he didn't fuck me right away. Later that evening, he dressed me in my good black dress and my garter belt and stockings and heels and pearls—and the harness filling just my ass with the largest shaft again. He fondled my breasts and rubbed and pinched my nipples, grinning openly when I let the trembling roll over me while I put on my makeup and did up my hair. Then he put on a suit and tie and drove us to a fancy club, where he led me, trembling, pussy juice and lube running down into my stockings, onto the dance floor.

I swayed against him, conscious only of the feel of his body against mine and the sound of his voice blending with the music. I didn't care who noticed the way I rolled my hips to enhance and capture every burning, stretching sensation as my asshole quivered in anticipation. I was aware with every step that the dilator stretching my sphincters was almost as wide as my husband's dick.

Almost. All I could think about was how when we were done dancing, Terry was going to take me back to our room and slowly, sensuously work the huge, smooth dilator free. Only this time, when he was done fingering my gape, he was going to open his pants and fuck his cock up my ass. He was going to slide balls-deep into me, and he was going to fuck me until the semen boiled up from his balls and spurted into my ass. And I was going to love it and him so much, it was going to make me come.

The night stars shone brightly behind us as he ushered me into the room. He'd set out a huge bottle of lube and a stack of towels beside the bed. He dimmed the lights, turned on music on the TV and set the laptop to record.

"Strip for me, Christa. Show me how much you want my cock up your ass."

I swayed to the music of my favorite band, slowly peeling the dress down over my shoulders, sliding off my garter belt and stockings until I stood there swaying in just my heels and harness and pearls. My nipples and clit were so hard they hurt. My pussy and ass were hungry for his cock.

"Please fuck me," I whimpered, rocking my hips greedily. "Please fuck my ass, Sir."

Terry growled and grabbed my hair in his fist, kissing me until I was shaking. Then he stepped back and tore off his jacket.

"Kneel on the bed." He yanked off his tie and threw it on the floor. His shirt and shoes and socks and finally his pants followed. He wasn't wearing underwear. His cock sprang free as his zipper fell over his hips. He threw two pillows in the middle of the bed and eased me down over them on my hands and knees.

"Spread your legs wide and put your ass in the air." Then he was in back of me, unbuckling the harness.

I lay there panting on the bed, clutching the sheet as Terry slowly, tenderly started rocking the dilator. The head was still wider than my anus wanted to stretch. His lips kissed featherlight over my back and around my lower cheek. My nipples were rubbing against the sheet, the sensation almost more than I could bear. I gasped as the dilator slid free.

"You have a gorgeous gape." His voice was so hoarse, he was almost choking. "God, Christa! You are so beautiful!" His fingers were slick with lube, caressing my anal lips, sliding knuckles deep, even the thumb, with no resistance at all. Then his hands were on my hips, and he was leaning into me. The warm, slick head of his cock pressed imperiously against my anal gate. For one ridiculous moment, my sphincters tried to clench, to squeeze and tighten and keep my lover out.

"Not a chance," he laughed, and slid in balls deep on the first stroke. His cock still stretched me. The long, deep stretch still burned. But it didn't hurt. It was just pure, delicious sensation, his stiff, glorious cock fucking me on a sea of lube and desire while I wailed and the first wave of orgasm rolled over me.

I screamed and came again. I was coming because my husband was fucking my ass. I was letting him deep into my body, holding myself open and vulnerable, trusting him to bring me the pleasure he'd promised as he finally claimed my ass the way we'd both craved for so very, very long.

We spent three days in Bismarck, then he got an assignment in Albuquerque. By then I was accustomed to the total body relaxation of having my ass stretched over dilators four times a day. I was also damn near addicted to the almost constant orgasms I'd been getting since I told Terry I wanted him to stay in charge for the long haul. He opened my dress and fondled and sucked my nipples, he fingered and tongued my pussy and ass, he fed me his cock and did pretty much whatever he damn well wanted to me whenever he wanted—or whenever I asked him to.

My priorities were redefined exactly the way I wanted them to be, and I was happier than I'd ever been—all because I gave my husband permission to take my ass and make it his. And he did it. I couldn't wait for him to buckle me into my harness, put me in my seat belt and get us back on the road.

BETTER THAN A MASSAGE

Annabeth Leong

Teresa didn't want to interrupt Carla's sleep. She tried not to fidget.

Nothing could defeat the dreadful thoughts that always came in the middle of the night. What had she become? Transformed from respected wife to couch-surfing mess, working full time but still not making ends meet, depressed and getting judged for it by most of her friends. How could she have chosen these things for herself?

"Teresa?" Sleep slurred Carla's words. "Your foot keeps tapping my leg."

"Shit, sorry." Her feet always got going at the same time as her nerves. Teresa focused on her breathing, working to make it slow and normal.

Beside her, Carla sighed. "You can't sleep again."

"I didn't mean to—"

"I know you didn't wake me up on purpose. Waves of stress are just pouring off you." Carla rolled toward Teresa, her features soft and hazy in the dim bedroom. The covers slipped off her shoulder, revealing the curve of a breast, a copper-colored nipple.

Still in awe of their nakedness together, Teresa lifted a hand, cupping the side of Carla's face and sliding to the downy hairs on the back of her neck. She couldn't resist going after that exposed breast, shifting so she could lift it in her palm and tease the nipple with the point of her thumbnail. She punctuated the gesture with a kiss and grinned at Carla.

"If you're going to be like that about it, I guess I'll have to forgive you." Carla caught the back of Teresa's head, pulling her tighter against her chest.

Sex seemed like a good reason to lose sleep—much better than worry and self-recrimination. That was, after all, why Teresa had first started these sleepovers with Carla. She put a hand on her friend's warm stomach and caressed her way down, hoping to find moisture waiting between Carla's legs.

Jackpot. Carla moaned and spread herself. Teresa stroked patiently, finding Carla's clit but also taking time to pull lightly on her stretchy inner lips, to smooth her wetness over skin it hadn't yet reached, to feel around Carla's hole and run fingers along the inside of her every fold.

Carla responded to all of it, bucking her hips and grunting encouragement, and finally grabbing Teresa's hand and guiding it to exactly the places she wanted to be touched. She came hard and easily, inspiring equal parts jealousy and admiration in Teresa.

"Thank you," Carla said. She kissed the top of Teresa's breast. "You are my very best friend with benefits."

Teresa smiled wryly in the dark. Carla meant affection, but Teresa couldn't help hearing the endearment as a demotion. She used to be somebody's wife. Again, she tried to hide her mood, but Carla picked up the change as easily as she'd picked up Teresa herself. "You've gone all stiff again. You need to get fucked in the ass or something."

Teresa couldn't help but laugh, shaking her head. "What?"

"I'm serious! It's totally relaxing. Better than a massage."

"You'll forgive me if I'm skeptical."

"What? Really?" Carla pulled away, lifting herself up on an elbow. Teresa winced at the sudden surge of lust that passed through her. Her feelings about Carla's body sealed the image of herself as immature, on the rebound and irresponsible. *Sure, I lost my entire life, but look at these great tits I get to feel!* Teresa scowled.

Before Teresa could get too deep into self-pity, Carla pulled her back to reality. "Have you never been fucked in the ass?" she demanded, pinching Teresa on the body part in question.

"No, I have." Teresa batted Carla's hand out of the way. "Nothing relaxing about it." She closed her eyes, stomach suddenly churning. "When I tried to talk to Brandon about spicing up our sex life, that kind of thing was all he wanted. Let him fuck me in the ass, have a threesome with him and a *Playboy* bunny. It's standard male fantasy stuff. I don't think the woman's supposed to get anything out of it."

"Would he totally cream his pants if he saw you with me, or what?"

Teresa shifted, putting some distance between herself and Carla. She didn't like thinking about Brandon. "Probably. I guess."

Carla sat up cross-legged on the bed and draped one of the blankets around her shoulders. "But you like what we do, right? For you?"

"Of course! I—"

"I have a point. Maybe the problem was Brandon didn't

present his fantasies the best way. You would have loved to make out with a hot chick, right?"

"Yeah," Teresa admitted, remembering the thoughts she'd had about Carla long before she'd even thought of leaving Brandon.

"And he would have liked to watch. If you guys had been getting along, it might have worked."

"Maybe." Teresa frowned. Conversations like this inevitably made her feel she should have tried harder.

"Don't worry about him," Carla said, reaching over to rub Teresa's arm. "I'm just trying to tell you the ass is the same—there's plenty in it for you."

"Isn't it about him shoving his cock in somewhere really tight? I'm not into that."

"Maybe he had a selfish fantasy about it, but I can tell you that after I get fucked in the ass, I get the best sleep of my life. Like I just spent a week at the spa. I swear." Carla grinned wickedly. "The ass is about your lover spending hours opening you up. Seducing you. Pleasuring you very slowly. It's holiday sex, because you need the whole damn day."

Despite herself, Teresa felt a surge of blood to her clit. She studied Carla. The other woman seemed so different from herself—free rather than repressed, light where Teresa was dark, voluptuous rather than slim, sexy rather than awkward. Easy on the eyes and easy with her pleasure. Trusting Carla had led to more fun than Teresa had ever had in her life. She bit her lip.

"Okay," she said.

"Okay, what?" Carla cocked her head.

Teresa blushed furiously, glad for the dark. "Okay, you can fuck my ass? You were trying to convince me, right?"

"Me?"

"Who else?"

"Uh, someone with a cock?"

"I thought you said it wasn't about shoving it in somewhere really tight?" Teresa sat up suddenly, putting her arms around Carla. Tears rushed to her eyes, and she pushed them away by kissing the tip of Carla's ear. "You're the only one I'd want to try it with."

Carla wasn't fooled by the kiss. She caught a tear on her fingertip. "I've never...been the top before. You sure you want to? It's not like I need—"

Teresa interrupted her, kissing Carla hard and crushing their breasts together. "I want you to seduce me every way you possibly can," she whispered against Carla's mouth. Her voice shook. "I want to give you everything."

Carla stayed quiet long enough for Teresa to worry she'd freaked her friend out. "I mean," Teresa said, "only if you want to."

"Oh, I want to." Carla seemed dazed. She kissed her way down Teresa's body and buried her face between her legs. "You're soaking," Carla breathed, knowing the customary shyness of Teresa's cunt.

"Lick me," Teresa begged, and went on to be amazed by how fast she came.

Freshly showered, dressed as if for yoga class, Teresa showed up at Carla's place late the next Saturday morning. "I've got to get my own apartment," she told her friend. "Marie's cats are killing me."

Carla clucked sympathetically. Teresa would have continued her complaints, but she trailed off at the sight of Carla's bed. "Wow, this is a lot of technology." A massage bar. A special pump bottle of lube. A string of silicone beads with a big handle at the end. A lipstick vibe. A strap-on she'd never seen before.

"I told you I would take my time with you," Carla said. "I meant it."

"Where did all this come from?"

Carla put her hands on Teresa's waist and guided her to the bed. "I wanted this to be perfect for you. And I may have gotten a little carried away at the toy store."

Teresa grinned. "Are you nervous?"

"No."

Teresa sighed and pressed the side of her face against Carla's stomach. "Okay, maybe," Carla conceded.

"You don't have to be. I trust you." The words spread warmly over Teresa's chest, like she'd slipped into a bath.

For an answer, Carla kissed the top of her head. "Listen," she said, "the first thing is we don't have to do all this today. If you're done after a bit, we can stop there and just make out."

"I promise I'll speak up."

"Okay," Carla said. She pulled off Teresa's top and bra, kissing her neck and circling her fingers over her nipples. "You start by letting me touch you."

Teresa took the cues Carla's hands gave, lying on her stomach on the bed and turning her head to the side. Carla pressed the massage bar between Teresa's shoulder blades and left it there until it warmed enough to slip down along Teresa's spine, a spicy ginger scent rising as it did.

The heat of Carla's hands followed, rubbing the bar in long strokes down Teresa's back, then setting the object aside and digging in.

Teresa wasn't used to receiving such focused attention—not without inspiring resentment in the giver, anyway. Several times, she half-started up, apologizing and offering to trade. Each time, Carla spread her hand flat, easing Teresa back to the bed like a startled animal. "We can talk trading tomorrow, if you insist," Carla said. "Right now, you let me do you."

Teresa breathed, stilled and tried to accept. The back rub went on long enough for her to fear it would end, then to wonder if it would ever end, then to give in to its seduction completely.

Eventually, Carla's fingers hooked the elastic of Teresa's sweatpants and panties and eased them down. One kiss on each globe of Teresa's ass, then the pump on the lube bottle clicked. The massage had done its work. Teresa just sighed as Carla spread her asscheeks and rubbed lube into the soft, tender skin there.

Carla didn't go straight for Teresa's asshole. She stroked along the insides of the cheeks and up and down the groove between them. When Carla did slide her finger to the hole, she zeroed in on a soft node of flesh there that made Teresa hiss and writhe as though it were a second clit.

"That feels good," Teresa gasped.

"You sound surprised."

"No, I trust you," Teresa said again, almost ready to come from repeating the words.

"Breathe out," Carla whispered. "Push against my finger."

Teresa obeyed. Carla's finger slid into her ass slowly, steadily, smoothly. Teresa felt no pain at all, only an intense, maddening pleasure that shot straight up her spine and made her start to sweat. She groaned.

"Hey, don't tense up." Carla pressed the lipstick vibe into Teresa's hand. "Use this. Keep yourself relaxed for me." Teresa fumbled and switched it on, then slipped her hand under her body and found her clit. The pressure of Carla's finger in her ass simultaneously sensitized her and made her orgasm feel distant. She panted and placed the vibe on her clit much more directly than she normally would.

Carla stroked Teresa's hair and back with her free hand and began to slide the finger in and out. She kept her pace slow—too slow. "More," Teresa panted.

Carla's finger stilled and eased out of Teresa's asshole. The pump on the lube bottle clicked again. A smooth, cool, thin object prodded Teresa's ass. "What is that?"

"The beads you saw. The first three are way smaller than my finger. They'll be easy for you."

Teresa barely felt the first two going in. The third made her sigh as it pushed past her sphincter. Carla noticed and toyed with her, slipping the bead in and out. "You ready for more?"

When Teresa nodded, a larger bead pressed against her opening. It stretched her until she wasn't sure she could take it, but then it popped through as well, making Teresa's muscles twitch around it. The muscles in her cunt clenched sympathetically. Her clit had swelled, so sensitive now that she kept the vibe on her outer lips. Carla teased Teresa's ass with an even larger bead.

Teresa keened. Carla's movement stopped. "You all right?"

"God, yes. More, please." Carla continued to gently increase her pressure. The bead entered Teresa with a jolt that traveled to every erogenous zone in her body—her clit, her nipples, her lips, her fingertips.

"I want you to fuck me," Teresa breathed. "I want your cock in my ass." She looked over her shoulder at Carla, whose generous breasts swung slowly as she worked the beads in and out of Teresa's ass. "Strap it on for me, please."

Carla frowned. "You sure? I can take my time and open you up some more."

Teresa shook her head, tears starting in her eyes again. "I need you inside me now." Teresa writhed on the bed, making the beads slide inside her ass. She watched Carla strap on her dildo, cover it with a condom, and smear lube over it with her palm.

Carla knelt on all fours over Teresa. She kissed the back of her neck. "Get on your hands and knees," Carla said, "so you can control how fast this goes in."

Teresa nodded. She hoisted herself onto her left elbow and knees, her ass angled upward toward Carla, her face puddled against the mattress. She kept the vibrator against her clit.

Carla gripped the strand of beads and pulled slowly. The erotic shock as each one exited her ass sent ripples through Teresa's entire body.

"You make me want to fuck you so hard," Carla said. The fervor in her voice surprised Teresa, who had been wondering if Carla could like this half as much as she did.

Carla aligned the head of her strap-on with Teresa's asshole and pushed in just the slightest bit. Teresa sucked in a breath. "Relax," Carla reminded her. "You can set the pace."

Teresa wanted to thrust herself back in one surge, to feel Carla's hip bones slam against the cushion of her ass. She forced herself to ease Carla's cock in a little at a time, pausing to get used to its penetration.

Carla patiently teased Teresa's inner thighs and talked dirty, just audible above the faithful buzz of the vibrator. "I want you to love every inch of this cock," Carla said. "Let me give it to you like no one ever has. Take my cock in deep."

It felt like a switch flipped inside Teresa's ass. The moment for care and caution definitively passed. She wanted Carla to fuck her to unconsciousness. "Fucking pound my ass," she begged.

Carla gripped Teresa's hips and shoved the strap-on to the hilt. She fucked Teresa hard, and Teresa howled and fucked back harder, almost falling in her enthusiasm to grind Carla's cock in as deep as it could go.

Teresa couldn't keep the vibrator in place, couldn't take herself over the edge to the huge orgasm she knew waited for her.

Carla's hand clamped suddenly on Teresa's wrist, locking the vibrator over her clit. "I can't," Teresa groaned.

Carla shoved her cock in as deep as it could go, leaned forward and wrapped her body around Teresa, slick and warm. "Come for me," she whispered. She played with Teresa's nipples while the other woman worked her clit desperately. The strap-on that filled her intensified every vibration.

Teresa's face scrunched up under the effort of tolerating the excruciating pleasure. "Let it all go for me," Carla said. Every muscle in Teresa's body strained and tensed. She arched back against Carla's chest and came, screaming as her ass clenched tightly around Carla's cock.

"I love you," Teresa whispered, too spent to analyze the words.

Carla kissed the side of her head, worked her cock gently out of Teresa's ass and held her as she dropped into a deep and boneless sleep.

Carla sat up reading when Teresa woke and stretched. After-noon light spilled onto the bed. "Oh my god," Teresa said. "How long was I asleep? I feel like I got massaged from the inside out."

Carla smiled, but said nothing. Teresa lifted onto one elbow, alarmed. "Are you okay? I wasn't—I wasn't too selfish?"

"You have plenty of chances to make me come," Carla said. "Don't worry about that." She sounded annoyed.

"I shouldn't have just fallen asleep," Teresa started. Carla laid a finger on her lips, followed by a reassuring kiss.

"Did you mean what you said? Right at the end?"

Teresa blinked. She blushed. Carla had been clear all along.

Friends with benefits. No way would she want to deal with the mess of Teresa's life. Surely Carla would have no trouble finding a lover who actually had something to offer. Anxiety began to invade Teresa's delicious, relaxed state.

"Did you mean it?" Carla repeated. "Or were you just talking to the cock inside your ass?"

"No!" Teresa cried. The hard edge in Carla's voice made her ache. "I mean, I was talking to you, not the cock. I mean, you don't have to—"

Carla's lips silenced her again. She reached around Teresa and gently stroked her well-fucked asshole, making her lover shiver and hiss. "And here I was worried that after all this you'd get back together with Brandon and break my heart," Carla said.

Teresa pulled back and stared. "There's nowhere I'd rather be." She hesitated. "No one I'd rather be with." The words felt true. Tears filled her eyes as Carla drew her close. In the cool buzz of her still-lingering pleasure, the muck of her emotions turned clear. She hadn't been demoted. She'd been set free.

BODY HEAT

Shoshanna Evers

Amanda Scott took slow, meditative steps as she walked up the stairs to her bedroom. She'd come so far since her first self-bondage experience, when she'd forced herself to wait until a handcuff key melted in ice before she'd set herself free.

Now she had friends. An online community who understood her, who knew what got her off. And it wasn't a man...it was herself.

Amanda could make herself come harder than any man (or woman—she knew because she'd tried).

Her experiments with self-bondage had become a hobby, something to daydream about and fantasize about at work. Tonight, she emailed one of her online friends—one who understood because self-bondage was her kink, too—to let her know she'd be playing tonight. Safety first, after all.

The Machine had been a gift from Joe, a very crafty man who loved to masturbate to private videos of her setting herself up in various predicaments. He'd made the Machine himself in

his basement workshop, and paid hundreds of dollars to ship it
to her house so that he could watch her use it.

Opening the door to her bedroom, Amanda pulled the sheet
off the Machine and grinned. It was a thing of beauty, if beauty
was thick leather restraints with timed locks and a huge dildo
that would slide in and out of her.

There were several ways the Machine worked for self-
bondage. Her favorite way was the timed method. She'd kneel
on the cushions Joe had thoughtfully provided for her knees
and wrap the leather around her thighs, forcing them apart, the
locks clicking into place.

If she needed to get out, she could just press the "open lock"
button, unless she set the digital timer. Then she'd have to wait
as long as the timer was set for before the locks would pop open
and she could free herself.

One would think having her legs restrained open with the
dildo fucking her pussy would have been enough, but devious
Joe also put hand restraints, so she couldn't change her mind
and reset the timer halfway through.

Just the thought of it got her wet.

There had been nights when she'd set up her camera on a
tripod, locked herself into place and set the timer for an hour.

A full hour of hard fucking (she could set the speed of the
thrusts too, thanks to Joe and his amazing skill) was a very,
very long time. The Machine didn't notice or care if she wasn't
wet anymore, or if it bumped her cervix and made her cry out.
It just kept fucking her.

She moaned, the memory tightening her nipples into hard
peaks.

It was rather dangerous, she supposed, locking herself into
the Machine. What if there was an emergency? What if she
really needed to get out and couldn't? She kept her cell phone

close by in case she had to call 911, but she'd never do that. The danger got her hot just as much as the Machine did.

Don't try this at home, she thought, and laughed aloud. That's what she always wrote when she told her online self-bondage forum about her experiences. Not like they'd listen. They just wanted to get in good with Joe so he'd build them a Machine all their own.

But Joe only had eyes for her, because she was hard-core into it. Just like him. The fact that he lived in another state and they'd never met made it even better, for both of them.

The other way the Machine worked for self-bondage was a bit boring, at least to Amanda. Joe had put a body heat sensor in the dildo, and she could set it so the locks wouldn't open until the temperature of the dildo reached body temperature—98.6 degrees Fahrenheit.

She'd never used that particular feature before. It wouldn't take too long to get to 98.6 degrees—maybe twenty minutes? It was fun, she supposed, if you wanted to be restrained and not know exactly when the locks would pop open. The uncertainty was kind of hot, now that she thought about it.

Joe didn't usually direct the action. He knew she was more devious than even he could be, that she found ways to torture herself that he would feel uncomfortable suggesting. Those nipple clamps last week, for example. Her tits still ached a bit from that one. In a good way.

Amanda stepped into the bathroom and took out a large silicone butt plug from her bag of toys. It was purple, and shaped in such a way that when she played with it, the tiny pointed tip pressed against her asshole, and she would push the lubed-up toy slowly in, gasping in erotic pain as the plug widened, widened some more, and then narrowed again to a flared base that couldn't get lost inside her.

Sometimes she liked to put the butt plug in before she secured herself into the Machine. Joe loved anything anal—perhaps it was his mild sadistic streak, since he knew her asshole was tight and virginal. The plug hurt on the way in and on the way out— in a good way.

Tonight was going to be different. Joe had made a request, and she would honor it, since his Machine had provided her so much pleasure. Tonight she'd use the plug, and she'd use the body heat timer on the locks.

But the plug was going in her pussy. And she wouldn't be able to escape the Machine until she'd been fucked in the ass long enough for her body heat to raise the temperature of the dildo to 98.6 degrees.

No lube was necessary, not on the plug, not now. Her pussy dripped with her arousal; the plug slipped right in, filling her cunt. She rocked back on her heels, holding the bathroom counter, and gasped as the plug hit her G-spot.

But the ass-fucking, that scared the hell out of her. If the butt plug hurt going in and coming out, what would a real ass-fucking be like? She'd never had anal sex before. In a moment, she'd set herself up in a situation where she'd have no choice but to go through with it.

Maybe she should play with her asshole a bit first, to loosen it up?

Joe would be pissed off that he was missing this on camera, but ultimately, this was about her, not him. That was the whole point of self-bondage, after all. So let him wait. She'd tell him about it later—about how she covered two fingers in KY Liquid and tentatively probed her ass, massaging the tight ring of muscle, sliding her fingers in and out until her fear of the Machine dissipated and was replaced by urgent desire.

It's time. My first ass-fucking, all by my lonesome.

Amanda grinned. All by her lonesome was her favorite way to go. Who needed a cock when she had a fucking machine? Who needed a dom when she had handcuffs and keys in ice and locks on timers?

In the bedroom, she turned on the camera and let it record. Once it was on, she pretended it wasn't there, that Joe wasn't there. He'd see from the angle that she'd followed his instructions: pussy plugged up, ass lubed, with a nice layer of lube on the dildo as well.

Oh my god, I'm really doing this.

Her asshole tensed in anticipation and she took a deep breath, kneeling on all fours on the machine. Reaching back, she secured first one thigh with the thick black leather restraint, and closed the lock, relishing the sound of it clicking in place, then the other thigh.

The settings were in order. She'd only be released once the dildo hit body temperature. Since she was restraining her wrists next (phone nearby, as always) and her pussy was now an unavailable orifice, she'd have no choice but to take it up the ass.

Adrenaline and desire coursed through her when she secured the final locks in place. The dildo wouldn't start until she hit the button, but once she hit it, it was staying on.

A quick moment of fear made her hesitate with her finger over the on button. What if it hurt?

It will hurt, and that's okay. Go with it. She could practically hear Joe's voice in her head.

Okay. Let's do it. Now, before I change my mind.

She pressed the button, and the Machine whirred to life with the now-familiar sound of the dildo slowly moving forward.

"Oh my god," she gasped, even though no one could hear her. Well, Joe would hear it later, but—

The dildo pressed against her tight asshole, pushing forward slowly, and Amanda bit back a scream. She tried to crawl forward without even realizing she was doing it, to get away from the dildo, to keep from getting her ass reamed.

The restraints kept her perfectly still, of course. And the dildo backed up, then thrust deep inside her again.

Erotic pain bloomed in her asshole, but the Machine filled her in a way she'd never felt before. With the plug in her pussy and the dildo in her ass, she was one with the bondage, one with herself.

One with the Machine.

She moaned, her orgasm building. Her clit felt swollen and needy, but she couldn't touch herself, not with her hands locked up.

Suddenly, the locks clicked open. Her body heat had set her free. But anal sex...even if it was with a Machine, was fucking amazing.

Taking advantage of having a free hand, she rubbed her clit hard and fast, her pussy walls spasming around the plug inside her. The orgasm crashed over her, stronger than ever before.

Oh, yes. This is amazing.

Now that she'd popped her anal cherry, so to speak, she'd tell Joe that his Machine could ream her ass any time it wanted—or rather, any time *she* wanted. Machines don't think, they don't want—they just fuck.

And that's the way she liked it.

Amanda set the timer, locked herself back up and winked at the camera.

WHAT YOU FEEL LIKE

Talon Rihai and Salome Wilde

C an I fuck you?" asked Spark, tipping his face up to Kavi's as they sat together on the sofa.

Kavi froze, from fingertips on laptop to baffled brain. He was as certain he'd understood the question as he was stunned by it. He liked to think of himself as open-minded. How else to explain a well-bred Indian exchange student falling for a spoiled American slacker? "I...don't bottom," he answered, flexibility hitting a wall, hard.

Spark nodded and turned his aqua eyes back to his book. Was his request really so casual? Kavi looked over, noting his lover had swapped Shelling's *Arms and Influence* for Kerouac's *On the Road* again. Unsurprising. The question should have been, too. Spark always chose what he wanted to do over what he should do. So different from Kavi, and a big part of the attraction.

He'd met undersized, strawberry-blond Samuel Patrick Arkness his second semester in grad school. They'd been paired in a political theory seminar for a research project, suiting neither of the loners.

"Kavi," he said with an offer of a handshake when they'd met at the library to begin work. Spark took the offered hand with an unreadable half-smile then sat beside him in the study room. Kavi's expectations—from sitting across the table from each other to an offering of the California boy's name—were dashed instantly. "Samuel, right?" he prompted.

"Spark," replied the slouching student. He'd brought nothing with him, no backpack, laptop or even a pen. He seemed barely able to keep his eyes open. Kavi sighed, realizing he'd be doing all the work to get the A he'd settle for nothing less than.

How wrong he'd been. Spark turned out to be a prodigy who'd graduated high school and college in three years each and was halfway through his master's work at twenty-one. Kavi was nearly twenty-four at the same place. But while the laziness and slovenly appearance irked the fastidious Kavi, the brilliant mind and elfin beauty wooed him like the California sunshine.

Within the two weeks they'd been given for the project, they achieved the A that showed they fit together intellectually hand in glove. And beyond the brain, too. In fact, they quickly found they fit together like golden-brown cock up tight, pale ass.

"Why?" Spark asked, tossing Kerouac aside and leaning his head on Kavi's shoulder, popping Kavi from his remembrance of those first strange, wonderful days that remained equally wonderful—and equally strange—after nearly a year.

Kavi took a deep breath and closed his laptop. A major exam loomed, the kind that Spark took in stride and Kavi stressed over, but he would be lying if he said that was what gave him pause. He enjoyed new questions and challenges, intellectually, but his preference for topping was something he took for granted, and liked that way. So what if his bond with Spark was different, was stronger than he'd had with former lovers? He was who he was. And, he had thought, Spark was who he was: a contented bottom.

Guilt hit him as his hand reached up to caress Spark's mop of hair. He didn't want to say no to Spark, a partner who, to his vivid memory, never said no to anything. From role-play and light bondage to food sex: nothing Kavi asked for was out of bounds with Spark. Together, they relished every new experience. Of course he would want to be on top, at least once. It made perfect sense. So why was Kavi so hesitant? "Why do you want to?" he finally replied, a stall he hated himself for.

Spark shrugged. "I'd like to know what it feels like. What you feel like."

Spark seemed to take Kavi's silence for an answer, and leaned up to push the computer off Kavi's lap. Kavi watched as Spark bent to brush his lips across his khaki-clad thigh. The familiar scent of herbal shampoo soothed Kavi. If they just stayed like this, could the question of letting Spark fuck him be forgotten?

Even as the cowardly question formed, Spark was turning over in Kavi's arms, lips parted invitingly. Kavi bent to kiss him, and Spark pulled him in. It was warm, deep and reassuring. When they at last broke the embrace, Kavi sat back, cock and breathing hard.

"Listen," Spark said softly, holding Kavi's gaze. "I love when you fuck me. I love when you say my ass was made to take your cock. I love the smell of your sweat and the taste of your come and the feel of your arms and ridiculously long legs draped over me. It's all good—better than good. And this will be, too."

Kavi shivered. He'd never spoken that way to a lover, never been spoken to that way. The directness, the detail. In fact, he'd never been with a lover long enough to find out if he might want to speak or be spoken to that way. But with Spark, there was magic. Hell, who else could make him blush like he was doing now? "Yes," he found himself whispering, consenting to more than he could put into words.

Spark easily turned onto his elbows to unfasten Kavi's pants. After a quick kiss to his flat belly, the slender, warm hands pushed his hips up and slipped pants and boxers down with smooth, practiced grace. Spark went immediately to work, cupping rich brown balls and gripping already-hardening cock before placing his mouth over gently retracted foreskin.

Kavi groaned at Spark's sucking. When he'd said yes, he hadn't expected it to happen right then, but when Spark took him in hand, the thought of interrupting fled what remained of his functioning brain. He groaned and, instead of gripping Spark's hair in his hands as he often did, he clenched them in the cushions of the couch and pushed his hips up.

It never took long for Spark to get a good rhythm going; they were so in synch that Kavi didn't flinch when Spark moved down from sucking his cock to his balls. After a questioning glance upward, Spark was parting his legs. Rimming wasn't new to either of them, so Kavi found Spark's hesitation merely endearing. He shifted his weight as Spark's tongue worked its way back to his entrance. This was as close as he ever got to being penetrated, and he gasped when he found Spark was working his tongue *in*.

His first reaction was to tense, but he pushed it away. How often had he had his tongue up Spark's sweet little ass? And it was a tongue, not...anything else. It felt...nice. Better than nice. He leaned his head back against the couch and felt his body flush with the pleasure of a damned good rim job. Thoughts of anything else left his head until it stopped, and he blinked down at a grinning Spark.

"Wha...?" he managed to grunt before he noticed the bottle of lube in Spark's hand. He swallowed hard. Spark was looking quizzically from the bottle of lube to Kavi's ass then to his face and back to the lube. Kavi couldn't help it. He smiled. "C'mon, trouble," he said, hauling himself off the couch and pulling Spark up. "It'll be easier on a bed."

Kavi impressed himself with how lightheartedly he whisked them into bed, watched Spark do a little striptease, then lay passively while he was spread and lubed, stroked and fingered. He had to force himself to stop holding his breath a time or two, but on the whole, Spark's generosity with the lube and careful, slow work with one finger, then two, left Kavi proud at how calm he was. It wouldn't be a total lie to say he was actually enjoying it, a little.

When Spark pulled back and rolled a condom and ample lube over his slender, stiff prick, Kavi had to fight not to close his legs.

"Easy, tiger," Spark cooed, voice as slick as his cock as he leaned in, pressing his head between Kavi's legs. "Just breathe."

He'd have thought Spark did this all the time, if it hadn't been for the way his tongue-tip protruded, like a kid trying to solve a puzzle. He watched Spark's mouth, purposefully and fixedly, as he felt the head penetrate. His teeth clenched and his eyes squeezed shut as the blunt cock worked through the tight band of muscle. "Fuuuuck," he spat.

Spark paused, but Kavi breathed hard through his nose and shook his head. "I'm good," he panted. If he stopped him now, he might never let Spark get to this point again. How many times had he encouraged lovers, encouraged Spark, to relax, to let him in? Time to take his own advice. His breathing evened out as Spark pushed farther in, then, slowly, almost wonderingly pulled back, then thrust in again. Relaxing was harder than it sounded, but the look on Spark's mystified face was nearly enough to do him in. "I'm not made of glass," he remarked, breathlessly. "You doing okay in there?"

Spark seemed surprised to be asked the question and nodded hastily. Kavi could easily guess he was so focused on being careful that he wasn't yet thinking about his own pleasure. But this was Spark, and pleasure was what it was all about. "It's... tight," he said, wrinkling his brow. "Can I go faster?"

"I don't know, can you?" Kavi teased. He reached up to stroke Spark's cheek. "Add a little more lube and try speeding up a bit. Keep the rhythm steady so he—so I," he amended quickly, "can get used to it."

Spark nodded, biting his lip, and did as prompted. Soon Kavi was lubed enough and Spark was steady enough to let them both be silent awhile and just feel. There was no denying it was interesting, and soon it didn't hurt much at all, but not hurting wasn't the same as mind-blowingly awesome, which was what fucking Spark was.

Looking up, he noticed Spark's expression was serious as he drove in and out, and as his body was rocked, Kavi couldn't help but wonder if he'd ever looked like that. With so much experience—with his many former short-term boyfriends back in India, the one or two since starting at UCLA, and now Spark—he was sure it had been some time since sex was something to look worried over. "Is it good?" he prompted.

Spark stopped humping and frowned. "It's...different."

Kavi felt a flush of disappointment. No, he didn't really want to be fucked, but if he were going to be, shouldn't it feel good to fuck him? "Should I put my legs around you?"

"I dunno." Spark wiggled his hips a little and pushed in farther. "How's it feel to you?"

"It doesn't hurt anymore," Kavi offered.

Spark's expression drooped farther. "When you fuck me, it's so good I can't even think."

"I know," Kavi said with a wicked grin.

Spark gave a one-note laugh and drove in hard and fast. It was how he liked it best from Kavi. And it did feel good then, taking his breath and moving his body around in ways he wasn't used to. He gave in to it, and wished it felt even better than it did...or seemed likely ever to be going to.

When Spark finally stopped, panting hard and dripping with sweat, his eyes were expectant. "Better?"

"Uh-huh," Kavi answered eagerly. He was still nice and hard. But he knew they both knew this wasn't passing the interesting experiment stage for either of them.

"I'm sorry," Spark said, shifting to pull out.

Kavi hated those words, especially from Spark. The solution suddenly clicked into place in his mind, and he wrapped his legs around his lover's waist. "Oh no you don't," he said, firmly. "You wanted to fuck me and you're going to fuck me. Good and hard so I don't even know my own name." He pulled Spark back down onto him and kissed him, strong, brown fingers gripping silky Creamsicle hair. Spark moaned into his mouth.

"First things first," Kavi said, when he broke the kiss. He reached down to pull the condom off Spark and rolled him onto his back. He grinned at Spark's confusion, then grabbed a fresh condom and rewrapped and relubed Spark like a present. "Very nice," he said of his handiwork. "Now up you get."

Spark obeyed quickly, scrambling to his knees. Kavi's already hard cock was even harder as he pushed Spark down to sit on his heels, then turned onto all fours while his lover watched. He turned to look over his shoulder and murmur, "Are you ready to fuck me?"

"Oh yeah," Spark said, voice thick with desire.

"Good," Kavi purred. "Now spread my cheeks apart. Like that. A little more lube..." Kavi could feel Spark's response to his every word, and every time Spark followed his direction he got a little harder. "Get your cock in my ass. Now." He heard Spark's groan, then felt the head of his cock against his hole. Instead of trying not to tense this time, he pressed back, feeling the moment, taking control. Spark let go of his ass with one hand, leaning over and pressing in. Kavi didn't let him hesitate and that slick, hot dick slid in like nothing Kavi had ever felt before.

"Oh fuck," Spark whined.

"Perfect," Kavi breathed, and reached behind to urge Spark over him, to grip his hair and pull his face down for a kiss. "Feel how hot and tight I am around your cock, bitch? Give it to me good. Like you mean it." He yanked Spark's hair and pushed back hard into every thrust.

Spark shuddered over him, and Kavi let go of Spark's hair to wrap an arm around his chest to keep that weight on him. The first thrust was hesitant and Kavi growled and pushed against Spark. He slammed in harder, faster, and Kavi's cock was suddenly gripped in a slender hand that knew it quite well. And then it happened. "Holy shit!" he shouted and his arms buckled a little. It happened again. And again. He saw the stars Spark had described, felt the incredible pleasure crashing though his body, knew what it was and didn't care that it made him the greedy bottom he thought he could never be. "Again! Right there!" Every push back, every drive into him rocked against his prostate and slid his leaking cock in Spark's hand. "Fuck me," he grunted again. "Damn it, bitch, FUCK ME!"

Spark seemed overjoyed to oblige, muttering, "Fuck yes," over and over, crying out as he dripped sweat and fucked Kavi with more stamina than Kavi suspected either of them thought he had.

Suddenly, though, Spark slowed, and Kavi roared his displeasure. "Don't you dare stop!"

Spark whimpered. "I'm gonna...Kavi...I'm gonna..."

Kavi couldn't tell whether he was more angry or thrilled by how quickly he'd made Spark reach climax. He wanted more, a lot more, and at the same time he wanted nothing more than to feel Spark come. His internal struggle was brief—a breath, a heartbeat—and it wasn't even a decision. He gripped the hand that wrapped around his chest, held Spark tight against him as he pushed into his hand and back against his cock. "Come for me, Spark." He was surprised but delighted to find he felt the same rush as when he was doing the fucking, a rush of elation, of gratification, of giving his lover no choice but to give in to his body, give in to his will. Spark would take the climax that Kavi insisted he take.

And Spark did. Shaking all over, his eager lover gave all of himself to fucking Kavi, thrusting and swelling until he burst with moans as desperately seductive as every time he came in Kavi's hand or in his mouth. He cried out his pleasure, kissing Kavi's back and clinging fiercely to his frame, while never stopping the stroking of Kavi's achingly rigid shaft.

Kavi drank it all in. Every sound, every touch, every bit of his beautifully bright Spark. He tipped his head back against his lover's face as he thrust his hardness into Spark's hand and gasped—just as he did when he was fucking—as he let himself tip over the edge.

Carefully, he helped ease Spark out of him and over onto his back, clasping the panting, shivering body in his arms. Spark's lips were salty but his mouth was sweet, as always. The kiss made him dizzy and the room spun a little as Kavi lay back, inhaling the heady scent of their bodies and his come. He was so awfully in love. Spark turned and offered his mouth up again. Kavi smiled and withheld the kiss just long enough to ask, "Was it good for you?"

HER KINGDOM
FOR HER ASS

Maggie Morton

present to you, Princess Bianca!"

This was her cue. The princess was practically shaking with nerves, but she knew this was necessary—it was this or her kingdom. And admittedly, her maid had been talking up the "act" for days, telling her how pleasurable it felt to have a man's sheath shoved up your—she could barely get herself to think the word—shoved up your *ass*. Prince Reece would be doing just this in only a few hours, and she hadn't even set eyes on him yet. Would he be hideous? She desperately hoped against it, but with her luck—her kingdom going broke after the war, her father's health failing—he would likely be even worse than hideous.

But as she walked out from behind the curtain and scanned the room, there stood the most gorgeous man she'd ever seen—lush, wavy chocolate-colored hair pulled back into a braid, a large, muscular-looking physique, and a face that easily could launch a thousand ships.

That face was turning toward her now, and he smiled at

Bianca—not a smile of lust, like she had expected, but a kind smile. *Maybe this won't be so bad after all*, she thought, smiling back at him.

"My lady," Prince Reece said, bowing to Bianca. She curtsied in return, blushing a little as she did. She blushed because she was beginning to wonder what the rest of him looked like, especially the part of him that would be penetrating her that very evening.

But first, there was a ceremony to go through—he was marrying her after all, on the one condition that she give him her ass on the night of their marriage, an embarrassing prospect but one which Bianca felt far less reticence toward after laying eyes upon this gorgeous man. Hopefully there would be more to him than just good looks, because she would be spending the rest of her life with him. It seemed likely that the part of their marriage spent in the bedroom would be enjoyable, but what about the rest? Would he be a bore? An—she smiled at the joke—ass?

But he proved to be no such thing, because as soon as the ceremony was over, he led her to a private room where their wedding feast awaited them. The fact that the room was private worried her at first—was he going to take her anal virginity right there and then? But no; instead he began to ask her about herself, as well as sharing tidbits of his own personal life.

He learned that she loved to read and ride her horses, and he told her that he was looking forward to seeing her library, and was looking forward to riding with her. Bianca learned that he loved to read as well, and he proved to be well versed in all the popular authors of the day. They got into a debate about one of her favorite philosophers, and she found heat filling her flesh as he showed her the sharpness of his mind. A sharpness which brought to mind another sharp part of him, and she surprised herself by telling him that they should skip dessert, and head straight to their marital bed.

"My, aren't you forward, my lady! My wife, I should say." And there was that charming smile again, a smile that she realized she was quickly growing to love.

She took his hand in her own and led him down the hall and up a flight of stairs, to a well-appointed, large room where a fire burned and a giant, canopied bed sat in its middle. This lovely room was to be their marriage suite.

Surprisingly, Reece looked a little bit nervous. "Bianca." He squeezed her hand. She turned toward him, waiting for whatever it was he had to say, and she took his hand to her chest, placing it right where her cleavage lay. She hoped the feel of her breasts would calm him a bit, and when he looked back at her, his eyes burned as hot as fire. "Bianca, I have something I need to tell you."

"Yes, Reece?"

"You probably think I have bedded many, many women, shoving myself into every hole of theirs I wanted, pleasuring each and every one of them until they just couldn't take it any longer..." Reece sighed, his fingers still on her chest, fingers that he slowly slid up and down the place where her breasts were shoved up against each other. "But I have not," he continued. "I have not bedded a single woman. And though I have lusted after the thought of fucking a woman's ass, especially one as round and lovely as yours, it is an act I have never performed before this night."

"Reece," Bianca said with a smile, "I am very, very happy to hear this. But," she said, closing the space between them and pressing her breasts against him, her lips only inches from his own, "I want you to end your virginity right now. I can't wait any longer."

"Neither can I," Reece said softly, and then he kissed her—her very first kiss, and possibly his first, too. And it was a damned good kiss, too, because it brought a wetness to her cunt that only her imagination and her own fingers had caused up until now, a wetness that was begging for Reece's touch.

But first, their clothes fell to the floor, piece by piece, until she finally laid eyes on his cock, a cock that looked to be just the right size to please her correctly. But it also looked intimidating, because it was going to slide into her tighter hole, the one she'd promised him in their marriage contract. The one that would be the first hole he ever penetrated, and Bianca found she was getting incredibly excited at the thought of them losing their virginity with this act. It was not one she had thought about much before the marriage contract was proposed, but now it was making her cunt wetter and wetter, merely by picturing what it might feel like.

And now, she realized, they were only moments away from their first experience with anal sex—their first experience with *any* type of sex, in fact. Bianca climbed onto the bed, getting down on her hands and knees, and she presented her ass to Reece, more ready to have her ass fucked than she'd ever expected to be.

She felt the bed move, and then Reece laid his fingers on her back, slowly sliding his hands down from her shoulders, until they cupped her ass, each hand squeezing one of her cheeks. Then his fingers dove in between them, moving down, down, until two of his fingers touched her asshole, a touch that caused Bianca to shudder just a bit, and she sighed as they began to circle her hole.

"Because of my research," Reece said, "I know that this can be a quite painful act; as a precaution, I had a wizard enchant me so that I would cause you no pain, so that you would feel only pleasure."

"How kind of you!" Bianca said, and smiled, which quickly turned into an open-mouthed gasp as she felt Reece's finger begin to enter her. It was the first thing to ever enter her there, and she couldn't believe how good it felt, so good that she found she couldn't resist shoving herself back against it. She heard a chuckle behind her, Reece's laugh suggestive and low pitched.

Then he added a second finger, spreading her just a little bit wider, and Bianca found it felt twice as good as the first finger had. She gasped and moaned and writhed against them, and then, just as quickly as they'd entered her, they were removed, and Bianca found the sudden emptiness quite unwelcome.

But only moments later, she felt something much bigger than his fingers pressing up against her hole. There was only one thing that it could be, and as Reece slowly shoved himself inside her, Bianca found the pressure and fullness of his cock were almost more than she could take, wetness practically gushing out of her as he spread her asshole wide open. She made her pleasure as clear as anything with the sounds that poured out of her lips, sounds that only became louder as Reece began to fuck her. The fullness and friction were almost too much, and then they were, as she found herself coming from the feel of Reece's dick fucking her ass.

Reece laughed again, a laugh that sounded full of delight, showing her that he had wanted her to feel this large, intense pleasure, another sign that placing her signature on the contract, beside his, had possibly been the best decision of her life. Because to feel pleasure like this, for the rest of her life, every night in their bed, was almost more wonderful than the fact that their marriage had saved her kingdom. No, it was even more wonderful—much, much more.

"You know," Reece said, not stopping his thrusts for even a

second, "there was a part of the wizard's enchantment I didn't tell you about."

"Yes?" Bianca stuttered, barely getting this single word out between her gasps and moans.

"He gave me the power to make you orgasm—to come—from having your ass fucked."

"You are a kind, kind man," Bianca told him, and then she cried out, because only a little after her first orgasm—the first one a man had ever given her—she was coming again.

And those first two orgasms were not the only ones she had that night; she came over and over again, and Reece did as well. They fucked until morning light came through the room's drapes, and just as dawn began to light up the sky, they finally agreed that it was time to sleep. Reece pulled the covers over both of them, and pressed his body up against Bianca's, his large hand gently cupping her breast. They fell into a deep slumber in mere moments, Bianca's exhaustion barely giving her time to thank the Gods in the prayers she always said before she went to sleep. As she mouthed her thanks for her good health and her kingdom's rescue, she found a smile on her lips, a smile she was certain wouldn't go away any time soon. Her last words of gratitude were for Reece, the first man to fuck her, the man who, hopefully, would make use of her other holes when they woke from their sleep. After she thanked the Gods for Reece, she finally fell asleep, exhausted, sexually sated and looking forward to waking up in her new husband's arms.

A TASTE OF
JAMAICA

D. Fostalove

Perched in the street-facing third-story window, Jamaica lit a cigarette and glared down at the pedestrians ambling along to the trendy eateries that lined the surrounding block. She looked over her shoulder at the wall-mounted clock and surveyed the men below. Her eyes focused on a portly gentleman, balding on the top, with a funny-looking walk. He wasn't Bart, or Beethoven, the lovable Saint Bernard, as he preferred to be called during their sessions.

As she continued searching the sidewalk and smoking, a loud pounding rattled the door behind her. Jamaica turned slowly and strode toward the noise. She read urgency in the knocks but was in no way rushed to receive the visitor. If there was one pet peeve Jamaica had, it was lateness, and Beethoven knew it. Her client list was long and the waiting list was even longer. Beethoven would have to pay dearly for his transgression.

There would be no walk down the hall to the elevator that

led to the roof where she paraded him around as if he was a prized pooch in the Westminster Dog Show. There would be no head rubbing while he ate his lunch from a black doggie bowl with a huge *B* on it. He would have to eat out of the takeout container he brought with him, in the corner, while leashed to the radiator. She would sit across the room, chain-smoke and chastise him for a spell before forcing him into the steel crate. After locking it, she would leave him there for the remainder of the session.

Jamaica pulled the door aside and looked toward the floor, expecting to see Beethoven already on his hands and knees in nothing but his undergarments. Had he been there, she would've put her stiletto boot on his shiny head and forced him to the floor. He had been a very bad boy and needed to know it immediately.

Instead a frail white man in an expensive-looking suit stood before her. "Can I help you?"

"Are you Jamaica?"

"Depends who's asking." She blew smoke into the air above their heads and tapped the ashes into a tray on an accent table next to the door.

"My name is..."

She didn't need formal introductions. Government-issued information meant nothing in her playground. Moving a few bronze-colored dreadlocks away from her face, Jamaica asked, "Who sent you?"

Her steely gaze forced him to avert his eyes. She had broken him in a matter of moments and would exert her dominance for the remainder of their exchange as she did with every other man who encountered her in the corner studio apartment.

"George."

She focused on his face, examining the laugh lines, the

furrowed brows, the dimples. "Is that supposed to mean some-thing to me?"

He lowered his eyes. She ground the butt of her cigarette into the ashtray before lighting another. He watched her replace the lighter in her bra before bringing the white stick to her painted lips. She snapped her fingers in his face, bringing him from his entranced state.

"Speak."

He leaned in and whispered. "He's a coworker who frequents your 'chiropractic wellness center' once a week. He likes…"

"I know what he likes." George spent most of their sessions crouching in the closet as he peered through the keyhole while she fondled herself to bukkake flicks. In other sessions, he would stand at the bathroom door as she showered, seemingly oblivious to his presence. He'd masturbate at a frenzied pace, hoping to finish before she realized she was being watched.

"He says…"

"I don't care what he says," Jamaica said. "I'm not accepting new clients."

"*Please.* I'll pay extra." His eyes were pleading. She'd seen the look more times than she could remember. Men who antici-pated the lash from an extension cord she had raised over her head. Men who wanted her to clench their balls in her petite fist until blood trickled from their lips as they bore their teeth into the fatty flesh. Men who ached to have her grind both stiletto heels in their chest as she stomped around the room in a fit of imagined rage.

"I can't be bought."

"Sorry. I didn't mean to offend you."

"Do you think I'm that easily offended?"

When he opened his mouth to respond, she blew smoke directly into his face. He closed his eyes but remained firm. She moved forward, yanked his tie and undid a button on his shirt. When she moved to put the cigarette out on his exposed chest, he flinched. She laughed lightly and discarded the fiery butt in the ashtray.

"Tell me." She paused. "What brings you to Jamaica?"

"I heard it's the best place in the world to be."

A growl drew Jamaica's attention from the man to the hall. She brushed by him to find Beethoven crawling toward them in boxers. His eyes were transfixed on the man standing in the doorway. His teeth were gritted as he cautiously moved forward. The man stared on curiously as Beethoven approached. Jamaica reentered the apartment to retrieve a leash that dangled from a nail on the wall near the door.

"Bad dog," she chided. "What did I say about barking at company?"

Beethoven whimpered as she wrapped a collar around his neck before snapping the leather strap onto it. The man stepped aside as Jamaica led her paunchy pooch toward the back of the sparsely furnished main room. Once they'd reached their destination, Jamaica yanked the leash hard before she knelt before Beethoven and scolded him for his tardiness. She threatened to remove him from the privileged lunch-hour slot if he showed up late again.

"Is there a bag out there?" Jamaica asked as she tied the leash to the radiator to restrain Beethoven.

"Two."

"Bring them inside and close the door behind you."

The man disappeared before returning shortly. He entered the apartment and met Jamaica halfway into the room where she retrieved the to-go tray from inside the plastic bag. She tore the Styrofoam lid off and tossed the tray of fried rice and saucy meat onto the floor near Beethoven. He looked up at her woefully to express his remorse for being late and his desire to have his special bowl. She pointed toward the tray and demanded he eat it, all of it, even the chunk of meat and clump of rice that had landed on the floor when she threw it down to him.

"Now."

Beethoven whined lowly and dropped his head into the tray, gobbling up its contents like he hadn't had a meal in days. Jamaica turned her back on him and glared at the man who was focused on Beethoven devouring his lunch. She cleared her throat and waited for him to speak. He caught the cue and moved his gaze from Beethoven to her.

"This may be a strange request..."

"Nothing you're going to say will shock me," Jamaica said.

New clients always prefaced their kinky desires with the line. It reminded her of a customer service job she held as an early twentysomething where callers always began the exchange with "I have a question." It was implied they had a question or they wouldn't have placed the call in the first place.

He looked toward Beethoven. "It's not something you tend to reveal in front of strangers."

"Spit it out," she said, no longer finding his intrusion on one of her high-paying patron's time acceptable. "What are you into? Diapers? Latex? Masks? Uniforms? Fetishism? Transvestism? *Felching?*"

The man looked at Beethoven, who had stopped eating to listen, and leaned in to whisper his request. Jamaica nodded and moved toward the end table that sat next to a leather chaise lounge. She pulled a small black book from the drawer and flipped several pages before stopping midway through it. She pointed a manicured finger at two different places on the page.

"Next Wednesday?"

The man shook his head like a pouty child.

"Friday? Yes, Wednesday evening or Friday morning." She tapped the corresponding spots on the page.

"Please, *Mistress* Jamaica, do you have anything sooner?" he begged. "You can do whatever you want to me. I'll be a total bitch for you."

Although a slight smile appeared on her face, she still waved a finger in the air. "No mistress. Just Jamaica."

"Yes..." He lowered his eyes with a nod.

Jamaica flipped a few pages and examined the scribbling on both pages in front of her. She let out a guttural sigh that sounded like a seductive purr. Beethoven lifted his head and began growling as he surveyed the room in search of the feline. Jamaica stomped to get his attention before she demanded he finish his food.

"I'll come whenever you'll have me."

"They all *come* when I have them." She kept her eyes focused on the planner, contemplating the rest of her scheduled sessions. Although the day had been particularly enriching for her, Jamaica really wanted to hop in her car after the last client and go home. "Call me around four. I'll see if I can fit you in."

"Today?" he panted, almost sounding as enthused as Beethoven, who had finished his meal and was ready to traipse the perimeters of her imaginary rooftop front yard.

She repeated herself and walked toward the door. Pulling it open, she stepped aside to allow the man to pass through. "Have a nice afternoon, Hampton."

"Hampton?"

"If she names you, she claims you," Beethoven said. "You're her bitch now."

"Good boy," Jamaica said in a soothing voice to Beethoven before shifting her attention to Hampton. "They say dogs are man's best friend."

* * *

Jamaica heard the distinctive beep in her ear promptly at four o'clock. She didn't need to retrieve the phone from the other room to know who the caller was. She pressed the small circular button to engage the device. "What a rarity it is to find a man who can follow directions. Don't you think, Hampton?"

"How did you know...?"

"I pegged you as the obedient type." She gazed down at her client for the hour.

He knelt before her, inserting her feet into a pair of patent leather loafers. She was dressed in a pink sweater with two blue stripes across the front, a pleated teal skirt and yellow undies. Atop her head, she wore a blonde wig styled with two pink-ribboned pigtails of spiral curls. Had she not been dark-skinned, Jamaica would've been a spitting image of the *Cricket* doll she'd fashioned herself after, per her client's request.

"Please say you'll fit me into your business schedule," Hampton said.

"Are we having fun or what?" Jamaica said to her client, mimicking the popular doll's catchphrase. She added an additional giggle for effect.

The man shuddered before her, a wave of ecstasy consuming his face. "Please say that again."

She repeated herself in the same singsong tone before she began speaking to Hampton, informing him of her weekly schedule. She held regular business hours on Monday, Tuesday, Thursday and Friday but scheduled clients between four and midnight on Wednesday for those who worked alternate schedules.

"I'll make an exception just this once," she said. "Be here at seven."

"Oh, thank you."

* * *

After Hampton arrived and all the business formalities had been taken care of, Jamaica told him to strip down to his skivvies and put on the apron that was draped over an upholstered chair. She retreated to the bedroom to change.

When she returned, Jamaica found Hampton in front of the kitchen sink with both hands submerged in soapy water. He was scrubbing a steel pot. She approached him from behind and stood on her toes to whisper in his ear. "I've been thinking about fucking you all day."

"Is that so?"

She gripped him at the waist and began slowly grinding against his ass. "I want it so bad."

"After dinner," Hampton giggled. "I made your favorite."

"Beef stew over rice?"

"Yes."

"How about dessert first, babe?" Jamaica kept grinding into him while planting quick pecks on his exposed back.

"I've been slaving all afternoon to prepare..." Hampton lost himself in her kisses and rhythmic gyrations, moaning lowly with each peck.

While she nibbled on his neck and shoulder, Hampton reached a soapy hand back and tried unsuccessfully to unzip Jamaica's pants.

"Is that really what you want?"

"Yes," Hampton whispered. "That's exactly what I want."

"Get on your knees and show me how bad."

Hampton spun around and eagerly dropped to his knees. Unzipping Jamaica's slacks, he reached inside and fumbled around. Pulling the appendage from its hiding spot, Hampton gazed on in amazement. "Geez, it's so veiny and big and black."

Hampton slowly stroked it, running his fingers over the

grooves and bulbous head of the lifelike toy. Jamaica loosened the silk tie around her neck and undid the top button of her shirt before thrusting her pelvis into Hampton's face. The black piece grazed his cheek, bringing a satisfied grin to his face.

"Put it in your mouth."

He grabbed the base and leaned forward, consuming the thick rod in one effortless gulp. Immediately, he began bobbing his head back and forth as Jamaica rested a hand atop his head, guiding him. She wanted him to know she was in total control.

"Open wider," she demanded. "I want to feel the back of that throat."

Hampton responded by grabbing Jamaica's waist and bringing his face forward until his nose touched the buckle of her belt. She was impressed at how easily he devoured the bratwurst-thick nine-inch dildo. He was no amateur. She then knew she could be as wild and unwavering with him as her heart desired.

"Suck dick much?"

He shook his head with a grin. As Hampton tongued the dickhead while masturbating, Jamaica grabbed a chunk of his hair, yanked his head back and forced all nine inches down his throat. His eyes bulged but he did not gag. She pulled away from him and jammed herself down his throat again, repeating the motions until Hampton's eyes reddened and tears slowly trickled down the corners. It was then she pulled away to allow him to catch his breath.

"Get up." She pointed.

Hampton looked in the direction of her finger. He jumped to his feet and moved toward the chaise shaped like a tilde. She instructed him to climb up onto it in a doggie-style position. He hopped onto the lounge and positioned himself as she'd requested. As she strutted toward him with the dildo sticking straight ahead, Jamaica could see Hampton's erection poking from the slit in his boxers.

"Want more?"

He nodded.

"Beg for it." She approached with the subtle seductiveness of a tigress about to pounce and positioned herself behind him. She slapped the dildo in her hand like a bat, creating a smacking sound.

"I need it *badly*. Please. Give it to me real good." Hampton bit his lip as he gazed over his shoulder at the strap-on. "Gut me."

When Hampton reached to pull down his boxers in anticipation of her invasion of his anus, Jamaica whacked his hand with one hand and ripped the fabric away with her other, leaving a series of tattered strips that hung loosely around his ass like vertical blinds. She moved the cotton shreds aside to take a look at Hampton's plump, lightly haired butt. She couldn't wait to penetrate him with reckless abandon and have him squeal like a bitch until his throat became raw.

Jamaica unbuckled the belt holding up her slacks and allowed them to slide down her legs until they rested in a heap atop her loafers. She spit in the palm of her hand, lubing the dildo before entering Hampton with no forewarning. He fell forward onto the chaise. She pressed her body onto him, leaving him unable to regain his balance. She slowly pulled the massive toy from his cavity before forcing herself into him again and again while he squirmed beneath her, his face buried in the chaise's smooth, dark leather. She could hear the muffled groans of pain and moans of pleasure as she stabbed into him.

"Isn't this what you wanted?"

"God, yes!"

She gazed down at him and noticed him biting down on

the leather. She grabbed his windpipe and squeezed without decreasing the pace of her strokes. "Bite it again and you buy it."

Instructing him to flip onto his back, Jamaica glanced at the pink KISS THE COOK apron Hampton still wore. She lifted the flap that covered his waist before lifting his legs in a spread-eagle position and plunging into him. Hampton's eyes rolled back. He tugged at his small, blood-engorged dick to match each of her forceful strokes.

"Deeper."

Jamaica wiped sweat from her forehead with the back of her hand and began tearing at the buttons of the oxford shirt. With each thrust, Hampton twitched below her. She pumped harder as she began feeling an added sensation from the pulsating dildo inserted in the strap-on's harness. Although she could feel herself nearing orgasm, she focused on Hampton and his need.

"Who owns this ass?"

"You do!"

"Scream my name."

"Jam..." he stammered. "I'm going to..."

She reached down with both hands and began lightly choking him as he continued jerking his dick. His head seemed to swell and redden. He gritted his teeth like an angry dog. As he began to come, she plowed harder. Hampton howled as foam spurted off to the left of the chaise. She released his throat and pulled out, standing unsteadily at the end of the lounge. Hampton went limp, one arm dangling over the side of the lounge, his head leaning toward his right shoulder.

"I've never been fucked so thoroughly," Hampton said exhaustedly after a few moments. "When can I schedule our next session?"

HARD ASTERN

Thomas S. Roche

There isn't much at all to that dress that Hannah's wearing, and Antoine's already gotten her panties off.

So when he gets down on his knees behind her, it's easy as hell for him to get his tongue up her ass.

But he doesn't jump *right* to that, of course. He's a gentleman. He goes nice and slow so she's begging for it by the time he enters her ass. He's such a gentleman, in fact, that he even brings his wife an extra pair of underwear.

What Antoine *does* lead with is this: he spirits her away from the increasingly raucous party in the main lounge of the *S.S. Petaluma Star*, where his engineer coworkers have been getting increasingly drunk on company-funded vodka and, true to form, are exchanging boasts alternately about their "elegant code" and their greatest achievements in World of Warcraft.

Although it's admittedly a sausage fest, fewer wives and girlfriends than you might think have fled the lounge, because drunk engineers can actually be pretty amusing. That means, hopes Antoine, that they'll be able to get some privacy. The capacity of the *S.S. Petaluma Star*, after all, is more than 130 passengers, and Geo Sprites Software Development has brought along no more than 60. The boat is pretty empty, all things considered.

It's this private little area and he scoped it out when he did the site visit: stern, lower deck, this cute spot near the rope locker where no one but the crew is supposed to go. But there isn't much crew on a nighttime cruise like this, and their only company is a Day-Glo orange sign emblazoned LIFEJACKETS INSIDE.

"Cold?" asks Antoine, embracing her from behind and wrapping his big arms around her.

As mentioned, there isn't much to the dress, but you'd have to have ice water pumped into your veins to get cold on the Petaluma River on a hot August night—even at ten o'clock, which it will be in another few minutes. Given what she's wearing—practically nothing, compared to what Antoine is wearing, a stylish wool suit—she ought to be asking him if *he's* hot, but on that matter, she's already weighed in by letting him get her alone like this, and he's weighed in by taking her here.

So Hannah doesn't answer; she just gathers his hands in hers and presses them tight to her tits, so he can feel the firm little beads of her nipples pressing through the too-tight dress.

She purrs, "What do you think?" and tips her head back and parts her lips and lets her husband kiss her. The rapturous little squirm her body gives as his tongue slips into her coaxes Antoine to slide his hands down the top of her dress and feel her firm little tits. Her nipples get harder by the moment, especially when Antoine starts pinching them.

When their lips come apart, he says, "I think this isn't from the cold."

And Hannah goes, "Ding ding ding ding ding!" like a game-show buzzer—sarcastic to a fault, even when she knows she's going to get fucked.

He pinches her nipples harder, drawing a gasp and a moan from her lips. With a dress this tight and skimpy and low cut and practically see-through, it was daring of Hannah to go without a bra. Why didn't she wear one? It's a fair question, but Antoine already knows the answer. There is, of course, the "pencil rule," where you don't have to wear one if your tits aren't big enough to trap a pencil underneath. Hannah is quite fond of citing that one as some sort of inviolable rule. But she only cites it when she wants to show her tits off. Hannah gets horny; she likes being looked at. She *really* likes being looked at when she has a chance to dress to the nines. She loves to dress up and show it off.

If he wasn't such an inveterate exhibitionist, too, then Antoine might be bothered by the fact that his wife likes strangers staring at her tits.

She also likes fucking in public, which is why he knows he can put his hands down her dress and only get a soft, moaning sigh in return.

He slides them back out of her dress, leaving the top pulled down and her small tits hanging out in the balmy night air. He brings his big hands down her belly, takes hold of her hips and grinds her back onto him, forcefully. From the open window of the lounge, they hear the drunken bellowing of his coworkers.

He pulls her hard against him, rhythmically, putting his full hot lips on her, trailing his tongue against the sensitive spot where her shoulders meet the back of her neck.

Hannah stays passive, gripping the railing as if she's been secured there. She loves the feel of her husband controlling her, holding her, taking the lead, telling her what to do. He doesn't *say* anything; he just commands her with his insistent weight against her, with his big powerful hands and with the cock that's swelling through his suit pants against her ass.

One of those hands travels down her front again, farther this time. From her hip, it finds her thighs; she's got them parted slightly, and the dress is really short. It's already pushed up a bit from the way Antoine has been grinding her back against him. It doesn't take long for him to get his hand up that dress and down into her panties; Hannah gasps and moans and bites her lip as Antoine starts fingering her slit.

She protests a little.

"Fuck," she says, still rubbing her ass against him as he finger-fucks her. "Antoine, what if somebody comes down here?"

"Shhhh," he answers, and silences her with his tongue. He kisses her deep, and pulls her tight against him, feeling her cunt get wetter with every stroke, feeling her clit swelling and responding more intensely to his touch as he kisses her deeper and works his fingers back and forth in her sex more insistently, penetrating sometimes and then focusing on her clit.

Whether Hannah's little protest came just because she likes playing hard to get, or whether she's really concerned, Antoine doesn't know—but he knows his wife, and she doesn't wear this dress to hear about World of Warcraft.

So he says in a growl, "You remember that thing we talked about?"

"What thing?" she moans softly. She's so dope-brained from pleasure she doesn't know what he's talking about, even after he's brought his right hand back from her pussy to her ass and worked it up her dress from behind. With his thumb, he plucks the back of her panties to the side. It's easy; there isn't much to them, so it's not much of an accomplishment.

Then his pussy-wet finger finds her asshole, and Hannah's eyes widen. She lets out an "Oh!" that he silences, gently this time, his kisses insistent but coaxing as he penetrates her with the tip of his slick finger.

By the time their lips part again, he's got his finger working fervently on her hole, and she's squirming against him.

"Oh," she pants. "*That thing.*"

"We're doing it," he says firmly. "Now."

"Right now?" she whines. "Right here?" She leans heavily forward against the railing and sticks her ass out, working her hips so she can rub her ass up and down in his grasp, inviting him in. "Right here in public?" she moans with a whimper. "No, Antoine, we couldn't possibly—"

His finger leaves her asshole. He pulls her panties down, sliding them over her thighs and then down to her spread knees. Her legs are just far enough apart that the panties arrest their natural descent; Antoine has to drop down and actively pull them; reluctantly, as if she hates closing her legs, Hannah puts them together so that Antoine can pull her panties over her calves, her ankles, her shoes.

"We couldn't possibly," Hannah moans again as her husband takes off her panties. One stiletto heel snags on the frothy lace of her panties and he has to disentangle it.

Antoine comes back up from his crouch, leaning heavily against Hannah with his pussy-wet finger back up against her butthole. He's got her panties in his left hand, out in front of her face.

With a quick sharp snap of his wrist, he throws them away, into the water.

Hannah watches her underwear spiraling out into the Petaluma River. There isn't even a splash when they hit, they're so filmy and skimpy. They just disappear.

"Those were expensive panties," she whines softly. "You dirty pervert."

Then Antoine's left arm is back around her, his hand down

the top of her dress again and caressing her right tit while he grinds his cock against her side and reaches into his suit-jacket pocket. He's got one of those little pillows of lube; he rips it open with his teeth, slicks up his right hand again and pushes his finger into her butthole. Her skirt has come down again, but his hand fits easily under it, and Hannah wriggles against the strokes of his finger as her hole opens up to him.

Hannah reaches down to press her palm against Antoine's cock; it stiffens more under her grasp. The slacks are soft and silky worsted wool, and the contour of his cock feels different than it does through the denim she usually touches before she gets his pants open when they fool around. The new sensation gives Hannah a thrill, reminding her that they're doing it in semiformal wear, here on a boat in the river with his bellowing drunken coworkers not far away.

His cock stiffens fully in her hand, and Hannah very badly wants to turn around and suck it. But she doesn't, because the moment she feels that overwhelming urge is the very moment that Antoine drops to his knees behind her and pulls her dress up to her waist.

Hannah's eyes go wide and she grips the railing as Antoine parts her asscheeks.

His tongue goes wetly and smoothly up into her crack; he never seems to mind the taste of lube, at least where her ass is concerned. She squirms against the stroke of his tongue as it wriggles into her butthole. His left hand's gone back around her; while he licks her ass, he strokes her clit. She moans in a sense of shock and filthy pleasure. As he licks ever deeper, his right hand wanders to her thighs and pulls her to his right, letting Antoine coax her legs open again until she's propped at a highly unlikely and possibly dangerous angle, with her tits against the railing, pert ass up very high, trim legs spread. She always hoped all those years of yoga would pay off one of these days, and with a husband like Antoine she's finding out just how frequent that payoff can be.

His tongue is deep up her ass now, the fingers of his right hand holding her asscheeks open as he licks in a combination of soft deep strokes and swirling circles. Ripples of pleasure pulse through her body.

Antoine's still got the lube packet, somewhere; he squeezes out more and his tongue is replaced by two fingers pressing into Hannah's asshole—gently, at first, and then far more insistent when her asshole resists. Hannah whimpers and tries to relax; it should be easy, with a couple of vodkas in her and pleasure radiating through her body. Even the awkward pose—vulnerable, exposed and shameless—can't keep her from wanting Antoine in her. But her powerful arousal makes her muscles slightly firmer, and makes her want it all the more.

So when Antoine insistently works two fingers up into her, she takes it happily. She even wiggles her butt back and forth, as if to signal her husband that he's doing exactly the right thing. He pushes them deep, and kisses her ass, reverent kisses as he starts to gently finger-fuck her, left thumb working on her clit as he does.

"Fuck," moans Hannah softly.

Then Antoine pushes two fingers of his left hand into her very tight pussy, never letting up on her clit.

"Fuck, fuck, oh fuck fuck, fuck fuck fuck," Hannah chokes and gasps as she grips the railing and snuggles her ass back onto her husband's hands, shaking back and forth. "Oh, motherfucking, fuck…"

Her voice is getting loud, almost as loud as the guffaws from the lounge far above. Can anyone hear her? Hannah doesn't care. She just keeps cursing in pleasure and moaning as her husband's hands gently but firmly open up both her holes.

Hannah's dress is mostly off of her now, both pulled up and pushed down. It's bunched around her waist with the straps stretched tightly out to her arms. Since the only other clothing she wore to the party was her underwear, Hannah's all but naked, the breeze caressing her skin as the *S.S. Petaluma Star* cruises at ten knots through the hot Sonoma air.

Then Antoine's rising behind her. Hannah feels the soft supple stroke of her husband's worsted-wool suit brushing up against her exposed back, her legs, her butt.

At some point while Antoine was down there, he got his pants open. His cock is out; she feels it naked against her butt. She reaches back to caress it.

He's got another pillow lube from his suit pocket. He brings it to his mouth; it cracks audibly as it breaks. A hot breeze comes up unexpectedly as he pours; he spills thin strings of lube on her two-hundred-dollar dress and his thousand-dollar suit. Neither one cares. He gets his cock slicked up, and Hannah helps him spread it around. He adds more lube to his fingers and returns them to her asshole, while Hannah guides his cockhead down between her cheeks.

His head presses in with only a slight amount of pressure; she's tight, as always, but she's also *very* horny for it. His fingers and tongue did the job impeccably; Hannah's asshole has never felt more ready for him.

She gasps as she pushes herself onto him. Her asshole accepts his cock in one firm thrust, and Antoine grabs her hair to tip her head back and kiss her hard as she snuggles herself more firmly down onto his cock. His tongue is deep in her mouth by the time his cock reaches its deepest point inside her. He puts his hands over hers on the railing and holds her against him as his hips start to work.

Hannah meets every stroke of her husband's hips with a backward thrust of her body, forcing his cock up deep in her asshole. She's already started moaning like she's going to come; it doesn't surprise her or him, since he did so much to get her most of the way there before he put his cock inside her. While his hips piston rhythmically, delivering deep thrusts up into her asshole, his left hand, slippery with lube, moves down from the railing and works on her clit.

It isn't long before Hannah cries out, moaning loudly as her asshole spasms and tightens around him. Antoine makes a pleasant sound in his wife's ear, purring, "Good girl..."

Good girl for coming for him. Good girl for letting him fuck her like this. Good girl for letting him do this in public where anyone might see...

Hannah comes hard; she keeps on coming almost the whole time Antoine pumps into her asshole. He can feel the spasms as he fucks her rapidly; he's already close himself. Hannah lets out the final sigh and enters the heavy slump against the railing that tells her husband she's completed her orgasm. An instant later, Antoine's thrusts take on an urgent quality; Hannah knows what's coming.

She positions her ass just so, looking over her shoulder and begging him, "Yeah," and "Please," over and over again as they lock eyes in the deep gray dark of the late-night gloom. He fucks his wife's asshole faster and faster, and then his eyes roll back and he lets out a thunderous groan. She feels her asshole flooding with him as his last few thrusts slide into her. Moaning softly, she wiggles for him, milking the last drops of come out of his cock.

Antoine kisses Hannah deep and hard; he pulls out, gets a handkerchief from his suit-coat pocket, gingerly wipes the lube from her asscrack. He tosses the handkerchief into the river to join his wife's discarded panties. Antoine zips up, buckles. He pulls her dress up, never taking his tongue out of her mouth as he does. Feeling the slick patches where lube has soiled her dress, he seats the skimpy garment carefully on her tits, her shoulders, her hips. He pulls it down over her ass, turns her around and brushes out wrinkles as he turns her around and presses her against the bulkhead.

His hand comes out of his magic suit-coat pocket again, holding a fresh pair of underwear, lacy and black but this time with a full butt.

Hannah smiles softly. Her husband. Always planning ahead.

She accepts the panties. With Antoine's arm supporting her, she steps into them and pulls them up her body.

Hannah lets Antoine lead her up the stairs to the main deck. She walks only a little more gingerly than before. They head toward the happy, cacophonous noise from the lounge.

IN TRAINING

D. L. King

This is so tight," I said. Sandy had finished cleaning the house about an hour earlier, had taken a shower in the freshly cleaned bathtub and was now lying prone on the massage table, ass up, with my gloved finger probing his delicate rosebud of a hole. We had a deal: he'd clean my house in exchange for anal training.

Sandy had answered my ad for a houseboy. I needed someone to clean my house twice a month. I could have hired a cleaning woman, but I thought it might be more fun to have a submissive boy who wanted to clean my house. Maybe wanted to clean my house for nothing in return other than the satisfaction of a job well done. No, don't laugh; I got some responses like that.

Let me tell you about placing ads for submissive houseboys: you get a lot of trolls, toads and general time-wasters. I got responses from guys who thought they could come over here, wear a maid's uniform, make tea and drool over my feet for a few hours a month. That's right, it was all about them. Even the ones who just wanted to clean my house. They wanted to do it so they would have Cinderella wank fodder. Now, don't get me wrong, I wouldn't have minded in the least, as long as they didn't decide to pull one off in the middle of my newly cleaned kitchen. But the thing is, when someone fetishizes cleaning, they seldom do a very good job. They become too wrapped up in their fetish and obsess over mopping the floor or cleaning the toilet. In the end, nothing gets done.

I just wanted my house cleaned—seriously. I was happy to pay for it. I wasn't trying to get something for nothing. I think the way I put it was that I'd be happy to pay the right boy in the currency of my choosing. The bottom line was I wanted a clean house when he left.

Like I said, I got tons of replies; many of them weren't worthy of a response, although I did respond, because it's polite. I initiated email communications with nine of them. From there, I whittled it down to four to meet and try out. That's how I learned about the fetishists. I'd given up and was begging friends for housekeeper recommendations when I got an email from Sandy.

He was the first to ask exactly what services I was looking for. No one else had done that. Promising. He asked how big the house was and how long I expected him to take to clean it. He also mentioned that he was afraid of heights and couldn't do the outside windows, but would be happy to clean them inside the house. Not only was he specific about the actual task of cleaning my house, the very thing I was looking for, but he could put a sentence together—in English.

After the preceding houseboy search nightmare, I was a little leery of beginning again, but there was something about his message. We began to correspond. He asked how I would like to pay him. I asked how he'd like to be paid. He had the perfect answer: *However you prefer, Ma'am*. He didn't have experience cleaning other people's houses, but he assured me that he was very used to cleaning his own and his friends considered him a neatnik.

I decided to try him out.

A week later a six-foot tall, trim, blond, gray-eyed, good-looking thirtyish guy showed up at my door. We sat down to talk. He had a day job at a magazine, he said, and would only be able to clean for me on the weekends. He said he'd always wanted to be sexually submissive to a dominant woman. I looked at him and he quickly backpedaled and said he didn't mean with me. He wasn't looking for sex. He would never be that presumptuous. I told him that was fine and he could count on the fact that I would not be having sex with him in the foreseeable future.

I showed him to the cleaning supplies and asked him to clean the kitchen and the downstairs bath, as an audition of sorts, then left him to it.

He did a good job.

I knew he would.

After inspecting his work, I brought him back into the living room, told him to drop his pants and then gave him a sound bare-bottom spanking, over my lap, first with my hand and then with a small leather paddle. When his rear end was a consistent, overall shade of red, and hot to the touch, I told him to stand and put his pants back on.

"Would you be able to start next Saturday?" I asked.

"Yes, Ma'am," he replied. "I could be here by ten, if that's all right with you."

Sandy had been coming every other week for several months and my house had never looked better. Even my friends had commented on how clean it was and asked if my cleaning lady had any extra days. I told them I'd ask and conveniently didn't get back to them. If they asked again, I apologized and said I was sorry, I'd forgotten to tell them she didn't have any open slots. Only a few friends knew the real situation and, of course, they wanted to meet him. Which might—or might not—ever happen.

I'd been paying Sandy in a mixture of ways: spankings, canings, bondage after the house was cleaned, shackles while he cleaned, flogging if he'd done some special job, like cleaning the oven or the refrigerator. When we'd had a chance to talk a bit and get to know one another, I asked him if there was anything special he wanted to try.

"Well, I'd really like to try anal sex; oh, I don't mean with you. I don't mean I wouldn't want it with you, I just mean, I know you don't...you said you didn't, um, wouldn't...I mean I would never presume," he rambled.

"No, sweetie, that's all right, I understand. I know you wouldn't presume; you're a very good boy. That's why I asked you. And I think I can accommodate you, perhaps not with the actual act of fucking you, but definitely with anal training." I saw him shiver.

And that's how he wound up on the massage table with my finger exploring his ass.

My rules were simple: he'd finish cleaning the house and then he'd clean himself; he would dry himself, but not dress; he'd bring out the massage table, set it up, lay a towel on it and then lie down with his ass up and wait for me.

I'd watch him set up for our sessions. He had a cute, tight, muscular body and a nice cock. His cock would start to get hard as soon as he began to set up the table. I think he was slightly embarrassed because he'd race to lie down, hiding his budding erection, as soon as the table was ready. It was very cute, really.

This was our third session. I'd been fingering him and had just progressed to using my smallest anal plug. "Now, Sandy," I said, "you're the one who wanted to do this. Relax, sweetie. You're so tight." I stroked my thumb over his pucker and gently teased it, relaxing the tight clench he had going on. Lots of lube on him, lots of lube on my finger, and now, lots of lube on the tiny glass plug, which I finally managed to slide inside him. His ass ate it up and clenched around it for dear life.

"Raise up on your knees and elbows," I prompted. "That's right. I want you to relax and enjoy this. If you can't enjoy it, what's the point?" Keeping a hand on the guard of the plug, I reached my other hand between his legs and stroked his balls. He shivered as I gently stroked and pulled on his sac while I twisted the plug in his ass. Finally I could feel him loosen up a bit, allowing the plug to turn more easily. "That's good," I said. "There you go, much better," I encouraged him.

After the plug had been removed, but before I allowed him to dress, I asked him to follow me over to my desk. I pulled up one of my favorite websites and located the page I was looking for. "I'm afraid you're going to need extensive training, in order to ready you for anal sex," I said. "I want you to buy these." I pointed to the catalogue page that had loaded onto the computer screen. The product advertised was a high-end set of anal dilators. There were five in the set and they were made of a heavy clear plastic.

Sandy stared at them for a full minute without saying anything. "Um, when do you want me to buy them?"

I noticed his cock was standing at full attention. "Now would be good. Why don't you order them right now."

Without looking away from the screen, he said, "Okay," in a soft voice.

"Why don't you go get your wallet?"

As he was putting in his information, I said, "You'll need to get the harness, too." He looked at the leather harness, made especially for the dilators, and his very hard cock began to bob. After he'd completed the ordering process, I gave him permission to dress. "Bring everything with you next time." He actually missed his pants leg, twice, while trying to put on his jeans.

Two weeks later, I let him in the door and noticed the canvas shopping bag he'd brought with him. "I'm glad to see you're into being green," I said. "Today, we're going to do things a little differently. Get undressed and stand in front of the table." The massage table was already set up and waiting for him.

"Yes, Ma'am," he said. "Only, I looked at those dildos…"

"Dilators," I said.

"Yes, Ma'am, dilators, and, well, they're kind of big, don't you think?"

"I don't know. I haven't seen them yet. Once you're finished undressing, you can show them to me."

"Yes, Ma'am," he said, and handed me two boxes as soon as he'd folded his underwear on top of his jeans.

The harness was even nicer than I'd expected. "Let's get this on you first," I said, "before looking at the dilators. That way we'll be all ready to go and you can make yourself comfortable on the table." I fastened the waist belt around him and buckled it on tightly. The short strap hung down in back and the longer straps that would go between his legs hung down in front. "Okay, go ahead and have a seat on the table," I said, as I opened the other box. He picked up the longer piece, hanging down in front, and fingered it as if he couldn't figure out how the thing would work. Of course I knew he'd spent a lot of time looking at that site during the past two weeks. He knew exactly how it would work.

Inside the box was a lovely set of clear dilators, the smallest being only about an inch in diameter and the largest being, well, quite a bit larger. I held up the smallest piece. "This is nothing. We won't have any problem with this," I said, even though it was a bit larger than the little plug I'd used on him the last time. "Knees and elbows, now." Sandy got into position. I put on my gloves, lubed him up and began to tease his anus open. "That's right, breathe. There you go," I encouraged him. I added more lube to the tip and sides of the dilator before placing it at his opening.

As soon as he felt the tip, he tightened up again, but with a little more encouragement and talking him through it, I managed to tease him open just enough, and once the bulbous part passed his sphincter, the rest slid in easily. "How does that feel?" I asked.

"All right, I guess," he said.

I told him to reach his hand around, so he could hold it inside him while I removed my gloves. I watched him push against the base and rock it a little. "Feel good?" I asked.

"Yeah, I guess so," he said, with a bit of a question in his voice.

The metal clip on the short strap of the harness hooked into the open slot milled into the flange of the dilator. I brought the long strap up, between his legs. It was made with a V of leather in front, allowing his cock and balls to hang free. Then the V became a single strap that continued on between his legs. It also had a metal clip that hooked into a matching slot opposite the other one. Once both hooks were attached, I adjusted and tightened the straps.

"There," I said, "you're all set. Now it can't come out. Climb off the table and stand up." It took him a while to gingerly negotiate his way off the massage table before he was finally standing up in front of me. His cock was as hard as I'd ever seen it. I readjusted the straps to make sure everything remained nice and tight. "Okay, now you can clean the house," I said.

"Yes, Ma'am," he said. "I mean, do you think I can?"

"Of course you can." He reached for his underwear. "You can work naked today," I said. "That way I can check on you from time to time." His expression was delicious. The humiliation was an added little bonus to the anal training, hopefully for both of us, but definitely for me. His hand automatically went to his cock. "No," I said, "hands off. Once you get involved in cleaning, you'll settle down."

"Yes, Ma'am," he said, and went off to begin on the bathroom. He moved slowly and deliberately and even though, eventually, he got used to the harness and being filled, it took about an hour longer for him to finish the house.

When he was done, I had him bend over, with his hands on a chair seat, as I loosened the straps and unhooked them from the dilator. I gently slid it out of him. "Very nice," I said, playing with his newly opened anus. "How does it feel?"

"It's weird," he said, "but I kind of miss it."

"Yes, I know," I said. I handed the plug to him. "Go clean this with soap and hot water," I said. When he came back, I removed the harness from his waist and showed him how it worked. I put the small dilator into a little velvet bag and put it and the harness back in his canvas bag. "Next Saturday, I expect you to do this on your own. You'll wear the harness and insert the dilator and keep it in for at least three hours. You can put your clothes on over it, and go about your business, as long as you keep it in for the required three hours. Before you remove it, I want you to masturbate until you come."

I could see the thoughts going through his mind. That was the icing on the cake. He'd really wanted to do that today, but I hadn't allowed it. I could tell the prospect of coming with his ass filled was exciting him. I said, "Then, the following week, you'll bring everything back with you and we'll do it again. Any questions?"

He grinned and said, "No, Ma'am."

"Use lots of lube," I said. "And if you have any problems, call me and I'll talk you through it. You can do it. I'll keep the other pieces here. I just want you to concentrate on the first one." I sent him home.

I counted the days until our next session. I couldn't wait to hear about his experience; couldn't wait to make him tell me all about his orgasm. It would take a while, but we'd work our way through all five training dilators. And then he'd be ready. For me.

EVERYBODY KNOWS

Giselle Renarde

You know when you've just given a blow job and then you take the subway right after and you feel like everybody knows?

That's me, sitting on this faux-velvet seat, smelling like come and feeling so conspicuous I could hang myself. The scent doesn't go away. It sticks to your hair, doesn't it? And your skin. Sex is in my aura, gossiping with other passengers, telling them things that aren't true. I'm not a slut or a whore, though I've been called those names too many times to count.

There's a guy all in black standing by the doors. I know he's looking at me while I pretend to read subway posters. Every so often, I glance his way, really subtly, catching outlines of his bulky body. I imagine shouting, "What are you staring at, motherfucker?" but I second-guess myself. Maybe he's not looking at me. Maybe I'm wrong. Hey, it happens.

But I think I'm right this time. I'm pretty sure I'm right.

I turn to meet his gaze, but he's just staring into oblivion.

Suddenly I'm the one gawking at him...because I'm not sure anymore if he is a *him*. I look for telltale boobs, but he's got a vest on. Hard to tell. Smooth cheeks, though. Butch dyke? Maybe. Or trans-guy. I don't know.

And suddenly he's looking at me, right at me, and he asks, "What are *you* staring at?"

He doesn't say "motherfucker."

I replay his voice in my mind, decoding it, tasting its resonance. Looking down at my backpack, I cross my arms, feeling surly as hell. He beat me at my own game. *Shit.*

Now I'm convinced he's staring, but I won't look. I wonder what he's seeing, and my stomach ties itself in knots. I always do this. I get so self-conscious, thinking everybody knows—and this is nothing to do with blow jobs, not anymore. It's about *me*, about the essence of who I am. I get so sure people can see right through my present and straight to my past. Especially other transpeople.

Out of nowhere, I'm crying! What the fuck? I'm sobbing my goddamn eyes out, and this guy all in black swoops in beside me and throws his arm around my shoulder. I'm soaking his chest with my out-of-the-blue tears.

"Sorry." There's a pool of my snot on his shirt, but he doesn't seem to care. "Goddamn hormones."

He nods sympathetically, and says, "I'll find out soon enough."

And now we know, and there's something really soothing about being the same. The same, just in opposite directions.

Oh crap, did I miss my stop?

I ask him, "What station are we at?"

He says, "We just passed Dundas."

That's when I realize I'm not going home—I'm going *away* from home. I'm running away, at least for now. Kind of a stupid thing to do as an adult, but I guess I didn't get my fill as a kid. I'm always on the run.

He asks where I'm going and I tell him I haven't decided, and then I want to know his name so I ask him.

"Asher," he says.

I say, "Stephanie," and it's nice knowing he won't look at me with that cockeyed head-tilt. He won't ask what my old name was.

When he offers to buy me a cup of coffee, I nod. There's something really comforting about his big body. Just being around him, I'm so happy I lose my words.

They don't stay lost for long. When we get to the café, I tell him about moving in with Mike and Yaro. We were all guys back then, a Three Musketeers sort of thing.

"They were so cool about it when I decided to transition." I've never said these words before, not to anyone. "My family was *accepting*, but Mike and Yaro were totally whatevs. They just went with it, you know?"

Sheepishly, Asher says, "Not really. Nobody in my life *just went with it*."

I want to tell him what happened today, but I'm trying to get better at listening to other people so I shut the hell up while he talks about how his family thinks he's confused. And his girlfriend of seven years? She broke up with him because, as a lesbian, she wouldn't be caught dead dating a dude.

There's so much pain in his storm-gray eyes. He's huge, and still he seems beaten down, like the world won't stop trampling him. I don't really know what to say, or how to make him feel better, so I kiss him.

He pulls away, and I feel like an ass.

My heart is pounding in my ears, and I stare at the swirls of chocolate sauce on my fancy-ass latte. I always move too fast with guys. I jump in with both feet—except with Yaro and Mike. We were friends for the longest time, just buddies, even after I started my transition.

I guess it didn't take long before they were glancing at me. They thought I didn't notice. Maybe I felt it before today and ignored it. Sometimes you see what you want to see and make the rest disappear.

Asher hasn't said a word since I kissed him, so I talk about what happened. I tell him everything came to a head—okay, pun intended—when Mike had me in a choke hold…

"Oh my god!" Asher's eyes grow wide.

"No, we were play-fighting, wrestling, whatevs. I was kicking my legs, and my skirt flipped over my waist. It's not like they could see anything, but they both just stared. Then Yaro was like, 'Those are some heavy-duty granny panties,' which I guess is true, but they hold everything in place, you know?"

I look around to make sure no one's within earshot. "I don't know what happened after that. Yaro pantsed me bare-assed and…everything changed."

Asher holds my hand, and I take it as consolation for rejecting my kiss.

"I'm not saying I didn't want it," I assure him. "It's just weird. They're my friends, and here I've got Mike's cock in my mouth and Yaro's ramming me from behind?" I lean in close and admit, "I've never had a threesome before. It felt kind of…I don't know."

My lips are smiling, and I reach up to touch them. I close my eyes for a moment and remember the taste of Mike's salty-sweet precome on my tongue, and the brutal sensation of Yaro's cock warming my ass. He was holding on with both hands, holding my hips, a slow, careful entry, and then faster when he was all the way inside.

"It felt good," I tell Asher, keeping my eyes closed because I'm afraid he'll judge me.

His voice is a little gruffer when he asks, "So why can't you go home?"

I look into his stormy eyes, and I know that I've hurt him somehow. "It's like the end of an era or something. I don't want to be the tranny they fuck when they're bored or hard up."

"Tranny." Asher shudders. "I hate that word."

"Me too." I watch him sip his black coffee. He doesn't seem to like it.

He says, "I have a spare room, now that Jenna's gone. You can crash there if you want."

That's exactly what I want. That, and so much more.

To Asher, we're just roommates, but I think he knows I want a relationship. It makes me wonder if Mike and Yaro felt this way. Maybe they were waiting for the right time, just like I'm doing with Asher, hoping he comes around.

Every day on my lunch hour, I sneak to the home that's no longer mine and pick up a few things while Mike and Yaro are at work. Soon my bedroom is full of my stuff and I'm paying half the rent on Asher's apartment.

The guys keep texting me, but I don't answer. I feel immature for leaving the way I did, but I think it was inevitable. I also think it was fate.

Asher and I spend our evenings in front of the TV. He makes his own spaghetti sauce, and it's the best I've ever had. We talk about everything: about my giant clit and his tiny dick. We have our own language. Being with him is like being with myself, another self, another me. He's got different experiences, a different family, and I meet them too. They're civil.

On my birthday, my mom and dad drive into the city and

gush over my new apartment. They love the area, love the décor. They love Asher—they tell me that when he's in the kitchen sticking candles in my cake.

My mother asks if I ever imagine getting married. Usually the question would make my insides burble with rage, but as I watch Asher in the kitchen I know.

"What if he doesn't want me back?" I ask in a whisper. "What if he never comes around?"

My father clears his throat because Asher's bringing in the cake.

My mother presses her lips to my ear and says, "He's in love with you, honey. Can't you see it in his eyes?"

Asher looks at me and our gazes lock. I see it now, the depth of emotion. Suddenly, I understand the fear of abandonment that's holding him back.

After "Happy Birthday" is sung and gifts are unwrapped, my parents hug and kiss me and set off for home. It's just us now. As I watch Asher clear the dishes and wrap up the cake, I realize how much he cares.

"Do I get a birthday wish?" I ask, trying to be cute. Actually, I'm so nervous I could puke.

He seems tense, and I wish he would relax.

I laugh and say, "You've got icing on your thumb."

Grabbing his hand, I bring it to my mouth and suck the sweetness from his skin. His breathing gets all shaky. We're each as nervous as the other.

"Is this okay?" I ask, almost a plea, before taking his index finger in my mouth. This one tastes different. Not so sweet. My belly tumbles as I watch him, waiting for an answer.

Finally, he nods. "You're the birthday girl. How could I say no?"

His skin tastes like anxiety. It's a vibration between us.

I wish I knew how to put him at ease, but I don't so I keep sucking his fingers until his breath grows shallow and his eyes burn dark.

He pulls his fingers from between my lips and kisses me. Now I'm the one who can't breathe. I always imagined him kissing me softly, but this isn't soft. He cups the back of my head in one big hand and crushes my mouth with his. I can't catch my breath. His tongue is battling mine.

There's a warmth in my belly and it moves down my thighs as Asher backs me into his bedroom. He's neat and tidy and he doesn't smell bad, and I love that about him. I love *everything* about him.

It's dark, and he lays me down on his bed. His body is heavy on mine as we kiss, and his packer presses into my hip. His breath is mine. I inhale through him, and he gives me life. This is the kind of kiss I would die for. Asher is the kind of man I'd give my life for. I love him so much my heart feels like it could break all my ribs and burst through my chest.

"I haven't used a strap-on since…before." That's what he tells me, whispering every hot word into my ear. "But I want to fuck you, Stephie. God, I need to."

"Yes," I say. I'm nodding wildly. I feel desperate and I don't want this chance to slip away. "Whatever you want."

He crawls off me, and his bigness lingers on my skin. He's got so much body! I already miss the sweet crush of it, and I'm panting, desperate to find my own breath. Lying flat on the bed, I watch him open a drawer and pull out a harness, a dildo. He slides out of his pants. His shirttails hang low enough to conceal his bare ass. He faces away from me to strap on.

"I've never been fucked like this before." I mean with a strap-on. I've never slept with a trans-guy, either. This is like a million firsts rolled into one. I flip onto my belly and push my underwear to the floor, kicking it off. "I've never loved anyone the way I love you."

I hold my breath. I've said too much.

Asher laughs. He turns to face me, and all I can see is that dildo sticking out between his shirttails. It looks so real I could eat it for breakfast. He grabs it by the base and struts toward me. My flesh is all goose bumps when he thwacks my ass with his cock. I'm so turned on I almost forget that he hasn't replied to my *I love you.*

Almost, but not quite.

I can't wait any longer. I ask flat out, "Do you love me too?"

"Stephanie!" He shakes his head and runs his cock the length of my thigh. "Silly rabbit. Of course I love you."

My body is light as air when he drizzles lube down my asscrack. I laugh until I cry, because I've never in my life been this happy.

He tells me to spread my cheeks and I reach back, holding them apart, confident in the pink pucker of my ass. He presses his thumb inside my hole, and I echo his moan back to him. I haven't been touched since that day we first met, and I'm beyond ready to end my reign of celibacy.

His fingers play in my ass, stretching that tight ring like an elastic band. He finds the place that makes me groan and pets it gently, urging me to ecstasy.

"You've done this before," I tease.

He laughs. "I haven't."

Another first.

He says, "I like it," and my heart flutters.

Pressing his palm to my asscheek, he kneads my muscled flesh. His cock keeps smacking the insides of my thighs until he drags it up and sets the curved tip where his fingers had been.

I whimper, trying to stay open for him, make it easy. The more I think about it, the tighter I clamp down. I bury my face in his comforter and remember the kiss that started in the kitchen. I think about sucking icing from his thumb, and I taste that sweetness all over again. *Imagine if his cock tasted like that!* I envision taking it in my mouth, bringing it to life like magic.

My ass eases up, letting him in little by little. Asher takes his time. He's firm, but gentle. He treats me with care.

I'm getting hard, trapped between my belly and Asher's bed, but I don't want to think about that so I focus on the sensation of being filled. I gaze over my shoulder and watch Asher guide his cock into my ass. I can't maintain this pose long, not with both hands holding my cheeks apart. When I tumble down I feel him move past my assring. The dildo's cockhead pops through that tight stretch, and he's fully inside me now.

"Oh god." It feels so good I want to cry. "Asher...I've wanted this forever."

He says, "I know," and then, "Sorry I made you wait."

"Don't be sorry." I press back, shirking my body's resistance. "Be glad we got here."

"I am," he says as he thrusts gently in my ass. It's so good, feels so good. I press my forehead against the mattress and urge my body back until my butt bumps his belly. I love his big body. I love him so much.

"Is this good for you?" I ask as we move together, one body, one motion.

He says, "I just want to make you happy," which isn't a yes.

I ask, "What can I do?"

And he says, "Enjoy."

Then his hands replace mine on my ass and he reams me so unexpectedly I cry out.

He says, "Sorry!"

"No." I grab his wrists, holding his hands on my butt. "It's good."

He thrusts into me, regulated but forceful, hard. Shocking and sweet. I'm moving on the bed. I'm *moving* the bed! Every time I shift to let him in deeper or buck back for more, my belly strokes my sensitive shaft, my weeping tip. God, it feels so good, so good.

I hold Asher's wrists tight. I bet his hands are turning purple against my asscheeks. He fucks me relentlessly, unapologetically. He keeps at it. He knows what I want, striking the spot that makes the city lights more vibrant, that makes my heart more receptive to his love.

"Yes!" I'm pulling him down on me now, so his big body's draped over mine. "Please, yes!"

I want to feel him everywhere at once, and I do. We scuttle up the bed and he's all over me, crushing the breath from my lungs. This is it. This is the moment.

He presses his lips to my ear and his hot breath fills me with the words, "Let go."

And, god, I do. All the tension in my body floods his bed and I'm a puddle on top of it, soaking through the sheets. I'm nothing anymore. I'm barely a body. He's taken me and kissed me and fucked me into liquid love, and that's all I am.

When he rolls off me, he laughs. As I catch my breath, I laugh too. I can't believe this really happened, but I know in my heart it's the start of something new.

There's nothing to run away from this time. Everything I want is here.

WITH LUCY IN THE MIDDLE

Kathleen Tudor

Lucy, this is my friend, Jack. I wanted to introduce you, remember?"

Lucy turned politely toward her husband and his friend, and then remembered who he had planned on introducing her to tonight. "Oh! You're the—I mean—hello. Hi, I'm Lucy." She stuck out her hand, blushing. Jack took it firmly in his, shaking it once, holding on a little longer than necessary and winking before he let go. Lucy felt her cheeks flush.

"David says you were friends in college," she said, falling back on politeness.

"Yeah, we shared a few classes. And a few other things." Jack and David laughed and nudged each other like they were still back in college and Lucy found herself glancing around to see if anyone was watching. The group she'd been talking to when they approached had shifted and no one else was even looking their way.

"Relax, sweetie," David said quietly, putting his arm around her and pulling her close. "No one is reading your mind. We're just old college buddies."

"Of course," she said, blushing again as she looked up at Jack from beneath her bangs. He was giving her an appraising look, his eyes drifting up and down over her body, following her curves.

"You have a lovely wife," Jack said, not taking his eyes off of her.

"I've always thought so." He squeezed her and dropped his cheek to the top of her head for a moment, and Lucy relaxed into the familiar affection. "You two should get to know each other a little better. I'll go get some drinks. Why don't you chat?"

He moved away and Jack immediately filled the void with charming conversation.

But despite the good company, the evening seemed interminable. Lucy was nervous enough to chew through a leather strap, but the men seemed content to chat and socialize all night. At last they made their excuses, thanked their host for a lovely evening, and made their way to the car. Jack would follow in a few minutes and meet them at the house.

As soon as they arrived, David sent her to get changed. She emerged from the bedroom just in time to take a dry martini from his offering hand and greet Jack. His eyes were on her body again, this time fixed on her curves as if glued there. David handed him a rum and Coke and Jack took it and sipped without looking away from her.

"I think we've had enough social niceties for tonight. Do you both agree?" David asked. They turned to look at him, and he must have liked what he saw. David laughed, clapped Jack on the shoulder, tossed back his own finger of bourbon, and headed for the bedroom. Jack winked at her, took another sip of his drink and offered her his arm.

The martini was gone before they passed through the bedroom door.

Lucy tingled with anticipation, and her arm was warm where Jack held it. She had changed into a transparent purple nightgown that clung and accentuated and did nothing to hide her trim body, and if she ducked her head to peek, she could see growing evidence of Jack's appreciation. The thought made her go liquid inside, and her pussy tingled in response to her intense arousal. She'd been growing wetter and wetter since David had introduced his old friend several hours ago.

She set her empty glass on the dresser just inside the door and David swept her into his arms, pulling her gently away from Jack and devouring her with a hungry kiss. She opened her mouth to let him take what he wanted from her. She heard a hungry sound from behind her and whimpered in response, pleased that Jack was enjoying the view.

When David released her, she was dizzy from arousal. She stumbled, turned, and Jack caught her in his arms. He was naked, and his erection pressed firmly into her belly, long but not too thick, just as David had promised. He caught her face in his palm and she leaned into it, letting him tip her head back and devour her. His hand remained on her cheek, an anchor and a brand, burning awareness of him into her even as he held her steady in a world that was spinning around her. David didn't do that. He didn't kiss like this. The exotic newness was headier than the drink.

She nearly jumped when a pair of hands brushed lightly at her waist, but the smell of David washed over her, and the hands danced up her sides and plucked at her breasts even as his scruffy face nibbled at her neck and ear. She moaned into Jack's mouth, and then the tone of her arousal intensified as the hand not on her cheek drifted up under her nightgown to brush the abundant moisture at her entrance.

Jack groaned into her mouth and pulled back from her to rest his forehead against hers. She panted, then whimpered, as he lifted his wet finger to her lips so she could taste herself. "Fuck, David, feel your wife. She's so wet her thighs are soaked."

David's lips moved to her shoulder and his hand skimmed over her side and down to cup her ass, then between her legs. She threw her head back when he thrust his finger between her folds with none of the tender teasing that Jack had displayed. He dipped one finger into her and she arched back against him, her head on his shoulder and her belly pressing into Jack. She wasn't sure she could have stayed upright if it hadn't been for the way they both held her steady, their strong arms catching her as her knees went momentarily weak.

David chuckled against her flesh as he propped her up, then she caught her balance and his finger left her body. She heard him noisily enjoying her taste, but he was hard to focus on when Jack was cupping her breasts in his hands, kneading gently and rolling her nipples between his fingers.

She moaned and swayed again, marveling at how it felt to be gently caged and supported between two hard, sexy male bodies as they teased and pleased her. Jack bent to lower his lips to her aroused nipples as David stripped behind her. She felt his thick cock pressing against the curve of her ass and shuddered. "I want you," she said, not sure which of them she was talking to, or if she was talking to them both. She felt as if she were floating and spinning, confused and a little lost in space but aware—so aware—of every featherlight touch, every kiss, every caress of her body.

She let herself go limp and David (she thought) caught her in his arms. It was certainly his laugh she heard rumbling in the chest her cheek was pressed against. He laid her down and climbed onto the bed beside her. Jack lay on the other side and she closed her eyes as the dance of hands resumed, setting her whole body on fire with sensation and desire. David's hot mouth came down on her nipple, and then a second later Jack's lips sealed around the other and they sucked and teased in tandem, drawing the erotic fire to an even greater height. She reached between her own legs and marveled at the heavy pooling of arousal there.

"Taste her," David said. "She's amazing." She opened her eyes and saw him leaning back to watch as Jack moved between her legs. He lapped at her hole, cruelly avoiding the center of her pleasure as he forced his tongue deep inside her. She moaned, wanting to demand more and unable to call up the words.

But then David was kissing her and she couldn't speak anyway. His tongue invaded her mouth at the same slow, lazy pace that Jack teased her pussy, and she realized that they had played this game before—had practiced and discussed it, honing their technique. The thought made her moan and arch up into both of them. Jack took pity on her at last, lapping at her clit before sucking it into his mouth and flicking his tongue over it until she screamed while David swallowed her cries.

When she was still, except for a lingering quiver in her muscles, Jack and David both eased back and gave her a few minutes to catch her breath. She sighed and stretched, feeling as if she could melt into the bed.

"How do we do it?" she asked, glancing from one to the other.

"Well, it depends on how fast you want to go," Jack answered.

David said, "We can give you some time with just Jack to figure it out, or we can go all the way now."

"I want it all," she whispered. She felt as open and aroused and ready as she had ever been in her life.

David rolled onto his back and pulled her with him, guiding her on top of him. Behind her came the sounds of a condom being unwrapped, and then Jack knelt and pressed his fingers into her flowing arousal, using it to lubricate her ass. She tensed at first, but she quickly relaxed as his fingers probed gently at her hole. She had gotten this far with David plenty of times.

She pushed up so that she could look down at her husband, and she smiled. He was smiling up at her, his hand lazily stroking his cock. And yet somehow it felt natural that another pair of hands was touching her most intimate places. Then Jack's hands drew away and the head of his cock probed at her pussy. "May I?" Jack asked. David met her eyes for confirmation before he gave his permission, and Jack and Lucy both groaned as he pushed inside, stroking a few times before he withdrew.

"Precious," Jack said, and then his hands were on her hips, guiding her down onto David's cock, which David held ready for her. His cock was not long, but it was monstrously thick. Lucy moaned with pleasure as he filled her up, a sensation altogether different from the deep penetration she'd received with Jack.

When she had lowered herself onto his length, Jack eased her forward to gain better access to her ass, then his cock was there at the tight ring, and she tensed involuntarily. "Deep breath," he whispered, stroking her sides and back. David's cock pulsed inside her, and David reached up to pinch her nipples and caress her breasts, relaxing and arousing her. "Take a deep breath, then let it out slowly and push back against me. Good girl, just like that."

The words "good girl" sent a rush of pleasure through her and she moaned as she pushed back against him, wanting his pleasure, wanting to please him. His cock slid past that tight ring of muscles, with a sensation that was sudden enough to startle her, and they both paused as she got used to the feeling of unusual stretching, almost painful but not quite. Beneath her, David continued to reach between them to pleasure her nipples while Jack teased his fingers over the skin of her ass and back until she was no longer thinking of his cock penetrating her, but only of a desire for more.

Jack shifted his hands up her body, buried his fingers in her hair, and rocked forward ever so slowly, his long cock pulsing as it gained ground, sliding past David's thicker cock, still buried in her pussy.

It was several eternal minutes before Jack was seated completely inside her. Both men groaned as their cocks stroked together through her thin inner walls, and Lucy felt as if she would explode if they didn't start to fuck her. Then with some signal that she didn't catch, the men started to move together, one thrusting in as the other pulled out, alternating their thrusts deep into her body.

Lucy could only cry out with the pleasure as they penetrated her, each man groaning and gasping as they pleasured her and each other. The sensations were so intense that the focus of her world narrowed to the rhythm of their fuck and the tingle building tantalizingly behind her clit.

She ground into the light pressure of her clit against David's body, and cried out as a wash of pleasure tore through her like a flood breaking through a dam. Her internal muscles clenched hard and both men gasped as she gripped and massaged them in waves of uncontrollable ecstasy until first David, then Jack, cried out, caught up in her current.

Jack slowly slid himself free and moved away to get rid of his condom, and David took Lucy into his arms, where she lay limp with satiation and exhaustion. Jack returned looking unsure, and Lucy patted the bed beside her. He climbed in and snuggled up, his face in her hair.

"Would you say it went well?" David asked.

Lucy smiled against his chest. "Not sure," she murmured sleepily. "We may have to do it again to be certain."

KEEPING THE BRITISH END UP

M. Howard

Kate looked up from her lacework and cocked her head toward the window. *Crump.* She set aside her evening's contribution to her wartime wardrobe, got down on all fours and crawled over to the windows. *Crump.* She carefully poked her head through the makeshift blackout curtains. A blush of distant light down toward the Southend railway bridge. *Crump. Crump, crump, crump.* The rosy domes of light flashed brighter and took on orangey hues as they marched closer, following the train tracks.

Kate stood up, raised her skirts and hopped to the wall, undoing her garter belts on the way. She'd dressed to go out just in case the girls came by, but that wasn't going to happen—and now, timing was everything. She bent forward, braced her back against the wall and carefully rolled down her last pair of silk stockings while calling over her shoulder. "Mrs. Brown?" Things were so informal now that the War was into its fourth year. "Elizabeth Brown? Elizabeth, it's an air raid!"

Her elderly neighbor just had time to acknowledge Kate's warning when the sirens started wailing.

Kate hurried to her bedroom and squirmed out of her undies while adjusting her makeup in the mirror. A bit more lip rouge, and just a touch of color to the cheeks. There. She snagged her long winter mantle on the way out the door and hurried down the stairwell and into the street.

Now all the sirens were blaring—almost drowning out the *crump, crump, crump* of the approaching bombs. It was only six o'clock but between the low cloud cover and the blackout, the only light was from the east, where a hellish false dawn proclaimed the first Zeppelin strikes of the evening. Amazing how the Jerry pilots could see through that soup.

The streets were beginning to fill, but Kate moved ahead of the pack, nodding to the warden in his white-painted helmet as he waved her ahead with his dark lantern. "On you go, Miss, on you go."

Kate stepped inside the reinforced concrete entrance to the Underground, just past the gaze of the warden, and paused. Getting off in wartime London anymore was all about timing. When to hurry, when to dally, when to commit.

It wasn't like the early days, when Khaki Fever reached epidemic proportions. Uniformed lads off to war, all bold and bashful, having it off with eager strangers in trams, omnibuses, taxis, on the street—in the early morn, broad daylight and advancing dusk. Rationing and restricted travel took care of all that—and of course, most of the lads were *over there* now. Returning soldiers were either being invalided out or hurrying home to wives. Of course there were the Americans, but the young ones were far too brash for her taste, and the men were full of dirty French tricks—besides, they'd all been kept out of the City for the last few months, and all the girls she knew, herself included, were getting more than a mite peckish. Must be some big offensive in the works.

God, how she missed it all—that is, until the organized response to the Hun bombing raids.

Someone jostled her hard out of her reverie and she spun around into the arms of a dapper old cove in tweed overcoat and derby hat. "Oh, excuse me, Miss, are you quite all right?" He had a nice voice, with a touch of fin-de-siècle public school tempered by a lifetime of travel and private clubs. Kate lingered a moment in his arms, enveloped in his unbuttoned great coat and a manly fog of tobacco and port and masculine sweat with fading notes of lime bay rum. She smiled. Well, he wasn't all that old—maybe late forties, early fifties. He was just a mite shorter than she was, but when she'd spun about she'd raised up on her tiptoes, and once she'd settled down the height difference was negligible. Still, drat and double drat, didn't she just wish she'd worn her flats? He held her close and she could absolutely feel his hardness pushing into her lap. No, he wasn't all that old at all.

She ran her hands up his chest and applied slight pressure with her palms, smiling into his eyes. He was really warm. "I'm fine," she said, disengaging from his impromptu embrace. "I shouldn't have been loitering." She took his left hand in her right. "My name is Kathryn. Kate."

"Jolly good, Kate. I'm Herbert." He hesitated just a moment and smiled broadly, revealing a bit of a gap between his front teeth. He had clear blue eyes and a rakish, raffish little moustache. "My friends call me Bertie. Shall we?" He gave her hand a gentle squeeze and they moved off together toward the rear corridors of the bomb shelter, and a modicum of privacy. A modicum was all anybody needed nowadays.

Kate snaked her hand inside Bertie's greatcoat and around

his waist and Bertie did the same, hiking her skirt up inside her long mantel and over her naked bum. They were now at the vanguard of a well-ordered mob of Londoners surging down the dimly lit passageway. The sirens had stopped and the Zeppelin *crumps* were now felt as distant vibrations rather than heard. They'd reached the end and early arrivals like Kate and Bertie remained standing, occupying alcoves off to the right or left as the main body of shelter-seekers filled the main corridor.

Kate's back was to the wall and Bertie stood between her and the open corridor, with his hands in his coat pockets, spreading his coattails wide as additional cover. She was moist by reflex—had been since she'd entered the bomb shelter. She felt for the flap-fly of Bertie's trousers and undid the button. His skin was warm and soft, but his cock was big and hard. She peeked around Bertie's shoulders. The corridor lights were spaced a good five yards apart, but as luck would have it, the last light in the row, encased in a heavy glass dome and wrapped in metal basketry, was directly outside their little lovers' nook. No matter. Real Londoners had learned long ago not to see too much on evenings like this, and as for the newcomers and transients...well, who cared about them?

Kate shrugged off her mantle, folded it neatly and set it on the concrete floor. It was cold now but she knew from experience that it would be uncomfortably warm soon enough—men, women and children all packed tight together, sweating and steaming in the narrow confines of the improvised shelter. She assumed the position, planting her feet shoulders-width apart, and leaned forward, palms against the wall, but Bertie spun her gently around, drew her up, and planted a big kiss on her lips. How romantic! She kissed him back eagerly, hungrily—thrilled by his eager fingers on her blouse buttons, by his hot hands on her breasts and nipples.

Kate was just about to throw her arms around his neck when Bertie moved his hands to her shoulders and gently pressed her down on her knees.

Oh. Well. It wasn't as though she hadn't seen it before—or even done it before. But she knew from experience that if she was going to get anything out of this, timing was indeed everything. Enough to tantalize. Enough to excite. But nowhere near enough to—well, finish things.

She used her folded mantle to pillow her knees and looked up. Bertie was still hard, erect and horizontal, and was looking down at her with an open and benign smile, thank god—without the slightest trace of goaty satyr or nasty old man gloating. She grasped his shaft and tried to maintain eye contact with Bertie, but it was no good. He was biggish, but not *that* big and she focused on his belt buckle as she took him into her mouth.

Bertie had shoved his hands back in his coat pockets and spread the fabric out again as cover, slightly bending his knees to pump himself into Kate's forward stroke.

Crump, crump, crump. The Zeppelin must have completed its run and was doubling back on its course. Cheeky bastards. What the hell were all those antiaircraft batteries mounted on rooftops doing?

Kate was just about to disengage when Bertie pulled her to her feet, gave her another deep kiss and turned her back to the wall. He was wet and ready, and she was wet and ready, but just as she flipped her skirts up and over her back and was guiding Bertie in, the Zeppelin demonstrated that whether or not it was wet, it was definitely ready.

Crump.

The ground trembled and the lights flickered just as Bertie drove home. Kate screamed. A child wailed and a woman's voice crooned reassurance. *Christ.* Bertie had missed the mark and shoved it right up her arse. Now *that* was new!

The lights flickered on and off and Kate felt Bertie's hands grip her hips as he continued to drive hard into her. She bit her lower lip to keep from crying out again. He was bottoming out on each stroke and she tried to release her clenching muscles to reduce resistance. She could feel his balls slapping against her buttcheeks on each urgent stroke.

Crump! Crump! Crump!

God, he sure felt huge now.

Kate took their combined weight against the wall with her left shoulder and reached down to guide him into her cunny, but changed her mind. No. Not after where it had been—was still.

Bertie was grunting, "Unh, unh, unh," answered by Kate's involuntary, "Umph, umph, umph," and the Zeppelin's *Crump, crump, crump.*

As she scooped her hand down to disengage Bertie on a backward stroke, her fingers brushed her labia, and the thrill almost suppressed the outrage to her butt. Now that was the ticket. She rubbed herself hard, rocking back into Bertie's forward thrusts. Her breasts heaved under her blouse until she feared she'd do herself a mischief.

Crump!

The lights went off and stayed off. Bertie convulsed, quivering over Kate's back, just as she climaxed, a strange, distant climax, but a climax nonetheless.

Bertie disengaged and drew Kate up and around to face him. He hugged her close and whispered in her ear, "God, Kathryn— my little Kate. That was incredible. You are incredible." He stuck his tongue in her ear and whispered again. "Christ. I could get used to that!"

Kate reached down to retrieve her wrap, stood up to her full height, and kissed Bert on his forehead. "Don't count on it,

Bertie." She patted his cheek. "You know, Bertie, you got that last just a bit...wrong?"

The lights came back on.

Bertie wore a confused look. He drew his hand up to his chin, index finger along the side of his nose. He sniffed—and smiled. "Well, Kate. You know? It's all about the timing!" He kissed her on the cheek. "With any luck, they're out of bombs."

"All clear," shouted the warden. "All clear!"

It would be a while before the crowds thinned out enough for Bertie and Kate to return above ground. "Maybe you'd like to drop by my flat?" asked Bertie hopefully. "Why, we could wash up and—set things right? I have some marvelous old port. And..." he pulled a pocket watch out of his vest, "it is still quite early, even allowing for the blasted curfew."

Kate thought a moment. After all, Bertie was quite the nice old chap. "Bertie, love? You are absolutely right," she said. "It is absolutely all about the timing."

TWO-TIMING

Laura Antoniou

It's fair to say that since becoming the man I always was, I've gotten more ass than I ever did when I masqueraded as a butch dyke. But now the asses that wind up under my dick or suspended for my hand or over my face are more likely to belong to straight ladies. This is fine with me, since I'm pretty straight myself. But back when I started injecting oily bottles of testosterone and pumping iron and examining my chin for every new hair, I sort of figured straight ladies were going to want what I'll call a factory-equipped dude. I am absolutely after-market, even though I must say I come with all the latest options. So, for a while, I continued to date lesbians who liked the masculine side of things in a lover, and then some hot bi babes—because, you know, who can resist a hot bi babe? And that was cool; I wasn't in the mood to hook up and get engaged and married and be someone's husband any time soon. I'm young and hung and horny as hell and the world is full of beautiful women to pleasure.

One of my regular booty calls comes from Stella, a walking Craigslist ad. She is that frustrated housewife with a boring husband who goes off to work and hang with his boys, leaving her all alone, boo-hoo, and she can entertain. Why, yes, so she can. And far from being dismayed or puzzled by my new-made-man self, she was decidedly enthusiastic. "No spermicide, no pills, no diaphragm! Does that cock get any bigger?" was her gleeful response to my "don't scare the horses" pack 'n' play. In response, I pulled some gloves out of my fuck-kit and she eyed my hands thoughtfully.

"Do you prefer gin or scotch?" she asked, turning her back to sway over to the bar. I admired the view of her wide hips and the gentle arch made by her gorgeously tacky marabou-enhanced mules. Her shoulder-length deep brown hair was expertly highlighted with tawny savannah colors, her olive skin carefully salon tanned. Everything about her screamed tryouts for "Real Housewives of Portland," up to and including the moment where she licked the twist of lemon for my martini.

I wanted to fuck her so much it hurt. And we were soon humping on her Italian leather sofa to old-school Depeche Mode.

Did I mention she was a bit older than me? This only added to her appeal. I have always appreciated an experienced, horny woman. They are more likely to know what they want, and more likely to teach me exactly how to get them off. I treasure every one of these learning opportunities.

So, Stella would call me when she had an itch, and soon it became clear that her itches were more specific. I'm down with that; when you have a particular taste or fantasy or fetish, sometimes you don't open negotiations with it. You lead the hard-on to where it thinks the trail is and then you kinda push the sex-crazed tool into a new direction; that's the best way of getting something a little out of the ordinary. For Stella, that meant that her booty calls were booty specific.

I don't know what the big deal is around buttsex. It's a hole. Cocks and tongues and fingers and hands and dildos and vibrators and the occasional oddball rightly shaped object just *sitting* there can all fit in. Where they often feel good. Moving them around feels even better. Whee! More sex! Dirty? Well, what about sex isn't dirty, if you're doing it right? This is why soap and water and gloves and trick towels come in handy. And if someone wants to douche before the big date with my cock, I have no objection. I'll even help.

Not that Stella seemed interested in enemas. But boy, she does love a cock up her ass. Especially when she has a vibrator buzzing away at her clit. Or my fingers in her pussy or on her fat nipples. Or as much sensation as I could arrange for her. Nipple clamps came out a few times, freeing my hands to fuck her pussy and frig her clit while my dick was pounding up her ass.

It just doesn't get much better than that!

It was the nipple clamps that led to the unexpected turn of our relationship. Disappointing Husband Dave was frequently the topic of after-sex chats, sometimes over drinks, sometimes while waiting for the sweat to dry. Disappointing Dave, I opined one day, should be fucking Stella more often. Stella naturally agreed. "Well, why don't you make him?" I asked, dangling the nipple clamps. "If you have these, surely you have a whip to warm his buns and make him see the wisdom of warming yours."

"But Dave thinks it's his job to be the dom," sighed Stella.

"Well, clearly, he's not living up to the role," I said. "He's obviously waiting for you to put these on his man-tits and jerk him over to the bed and shove his face into your pussy. Try it one Saturday night and let me know how it works out."

Just call me *Dear Abby*. I'm helpful that way. Stella looked dubious and disinterested, but no worries. If the husband wasn't servicing her, I could always find time to pound her ass for her and work out those lonesome blues.

Weeks go by until I realize she's taken my advice to heart. "You know, I just shoved him on his back last weekend and sat on his dick and told him he couldn't come until I did, and he didn't!" she said with amazement one day.

"You go, girl!" I congratulated her.

And then another time, where we had to change the sheets on the bed because, lube, it just goes everywhere, she paused and told me how she was starting to get Disappointing Dave to be more cooperative by spanking his ass a little as her way of indicating she was ready for boning.

"Does he like it?" I asked.

"Well," Stella said, pondering for a moment, "it does make him hard. And I'm thinking maybe he really is more of a sub. But you last much longer than he does. He's still not the best fuck."

"Ah, well," I said, commiserating. "I do my best. But at least he's getting it up more, right? That's a plus."

Then, a few weeks after that, with the summer sun so hot it was too intense to stay out by the pool after I banged her on the picnic table, she showed me the leather collar, cuffs and leash she'd bought online. "You kinky bitch!" I said, slapping her fine, curved ass.

"Yeah," she said, running her hands over the soft leather. "But I wouldn't have known I had it in me if it wasn't for you."

And that naturally led to my wanting to find out just how far I could get in her, but this time, in the air-conditioning. I fucked her pussy first and then her ass and when I was riding her from behind, my hands on her huge tits, she started moaning something that sounded like commands to lick her. I decoded

1) I was not hearing her correctly and 2) even if I was, the laws of physics constrained me to my current doggie-style position. In any event, she came, I came, and nothing was said about licking.

After a lunchtime date in the early fall, while she was playing with the hair on my chest—damn abundant hair, I must say— she asked if I ever fucked guys. These sorts of questions might offend a lot of gentlemen of my persuasion; was she asking me about being a woman? About getting plowed in my vagina, now reclaimed and renamed my cockpit? But I have too many transfag brothers and bi-slash-pansexual buddies of assorted orientations to get hung up on honest curiosity.

Yeah, I admitted to her. I've been fucked by cocks and I've fucked a guy or two. Or three or four, actually. Sometimes, you know, the party is boring and the potential action is limited and you've had a little too much to drink, and well, I'm open-minded for a straight guy. Heteroflexible, some people call it.

Some people just call me a slut, and that's fine, too, if they say it with affection.

So I told her some stories about backroom fucks and how this one time a guy answered my ad and showed up dressed like a chick, and I might have been the first dude to actually fuck him and not take a swing at him. He had amazing legs.

"Well, I was wondering," she finally said, tracing a circle around my nipple, "if maybe you would like to come over one night and fuck Dave."

"I dunno," I hedged. My brain was going, *Oh, no way in hell, sweetheart. I've been fucking you for months now and you just want to slip me in to bang your husband and maybe he won't notice that we seem to know each other very well?* This could no way be okay.

"See, I've been fucking him," she said all of a sudden, like this wasn't the biggest newsflash of her married life. "I got a harness and a cock and he loves it when I fuck him up the ass, but you know what? I wanna see him get it from another guy. I think that would be really hot."

And what did she do, but pull out all this fag-romance porn stuff about cowboys riding each other and firemen fucking and pirates boning and even some what-the-fuck weird vampire gay sex picture book. Seems she's all turned on by two guys going at it, which seemed kinda weird to me until I thought about it.

I mean, I like to watch lesbian porn, myself. Two chicks and no dick means more pussy for my cock to be interested in, right? So why wouldn't a straight lady like to see two dudes banging, without a skinny, silicone-titted bimbo making her wonder if her tits are the right size?

Which, for the record, I must repeat—her tits were perfect in every way and just the thing to bury your face or cock in, any time.

So, yeah, I can see why she wants to see it, but maybe she should recruit some other guy for this? Someone not as familiar?

"Oh, but you're perfect," she purrs at me. "You can be just a little bigger than me and rougher and you won't go all psycho and think we're gonna be some kinda threesome forever after-wards."

These were good points in my favor. And to be honest, she was hot enough to make me believe I was the stud of studs, invincible and irresistible and when a lady has that kinda grip on your psyche, it's easy to get caught up in her fantasies and desires.

Which is how I wound up getting all dressed in my leather daddy clothes for a hot date with my booty call and her formerly disappointing husband, Dave. She wanted me to be all

dominant? Can do. Tall engineer boots, tight jeans with my best
fucker outlined so clearly along my thigh, you'da thought I was
smuggling salami. Big-ass leather belt, leather shirt, titty clamps
looped around one epaulet. Condoms, lube, gloves and attitude
to accessorize, and I was more than ready to play her game.

"So, what is he?" I'd asked her before we got to the red-letter
day. "Is he some kinda pussy boy, or a slave, or a faggot? Is
he supposed to like it or hate it? Am I supposed to be nice to
him, the nurturing, sensitive guy breaking straight ass cherry,
or totally fucked up and nasty, getting back at him for every gay
basher who ever sneered on the TV news?" It made her think, a
lot. This role-playing stuff isn't for pussies; you gotta approach
it carefully, make sure you got your part right. We agreed that
she'd call me by my full name if she wanted me to back off so
she could check in with Disappointing Dave. And I agreed that
when my part was done, I'd slip out so fast you'd think I had the
Lone Ranger's horse tied up outside.

She had him all warmed up by the time I let myself in. Oh,
yeah, she'd been topping the shit out of him, no doubt. Because
there he was, stretched out across the back of their Italian
leather sofa, his arms spread out to the sides and tied to the
front legs while his ankles were tied to the back. He had a big,
padded blindfold on, and I could see my clamps weren't needed
because Stella already had his titties clamped and weighted;
what a clever little minx she was! Riding crop marks on his pale
chest, too, and a very, very red ass.

Stella had kept her mules on, and I liked to think that was
for me. But otherwise, she was as naked as Dave, making me
very overdressed for this party. But image is everything. Stella
grabbed Dave's hair and jerked his head up. "I got a surprise
for you," she says, in a singsong voice. "I got you a real BDSM
leather daddy to fuck your ass tonight, lover. Fuck you so I can

watch you get reamed by a nice big cock, just the way you *really* want it."

Shit, that made me hard right there. I do love it when a babe talks dirty. She let Dave squirm a little and shove the edge of the blindfold aside, and I quickly stepped in close so he saw leather and hopefully the outline of my dick.

"But I want *you*," he immediately started whining, even though I could see his jaw moving and his tongue nervously licking his lips. "I only want you!"

"And what I *want* is to see you fucked," Stella said, pulling me in closer. I rubbed my crotch against his face, letting him feel my shaft and pulling his lips across the leather on my belt and then my shirt. Then I shoved his head down so he could get a good look at the boots—and yeah, that was the right move. Lip licking turned to outright drooling, enough so I got a splash of his spit on my boot.

I suppose I coulda done some sort of *Oh, now I gotta punish you* thing for that, but we agreed I was more a teaching daddy-dom type. "You think you can take my cock?" I asked him. "You think any virgin man-hole can take a real dick? You think it's gonna be like how you bone the missus here, all soft and wet?"

And I walked away while Stella adjusted the blindfold and he made more noises like he didn't like it. But his cock was so hard it was dribbling over the back of the sofa, getting that leather all slimy and wet. Not that he seemed to mind that, either.

I had to admit, the view from behind wasn't exactly something to inspire. He was okay for a guy, not too badly out of shape, and he was clean and didn't smell bad, but there was nothing about him that called to my cock. Luckily, Stella was there, tugging on his tit clamps while shoving her own boobs toward me. It was like she was dangling them just far enough away for me to have to slam my cock into Dave's butt so I could reach the goodies.

That seemed like a good game to play. But it could get so much better. "Come on over here, bitch," I said, grinning at her. "Get my cock covered and wet for your husband's ass, so it don't hurt him too much." She liked this and planted a big kiss on him before skipping around the couch to me and making busy with a condom.

"Yeah, I'm gonna get my dick all wet in your wife's mouth," I informed Dave, whose dong was perfectly happy with this although his mouth was making sounds like he was very upset. Stella was happy to gobble at me for a minute or two, but then we needed to get down to the real business of slicking his back door for my fuck. It would be nice if spit made great lube, but what can you do? Since she was more familiar with this hole, I let her apply the gloppy stuff. I worked my dick as she finger-fucked her husband, getting a healthy amount of the stuff up his hole.

She asked him if he was ready for his first taste of man-cock, and he swore he'd love no cock but hers. That seemed to be the time to get him acquainted with mine, and I told her to put me in him. "Yeah," I said, "I'm not gonna just fuck him because you said so. You gotta get me in there and while you're down there, squeeze his balls and kiss mine."

He liked that so much he started humping away like there was a pussy under him. Actually aiming for that moving hole did require some focus, but with Stella's help, I got the head in, and the rest was like sliding home. This man wasn't just ready for cock, he was hungry for it. His ass swallowed me with as much suction as her mouth could, and it was so surprising I almost gasped out loud. Suddenly, my growling at him to take my big cock seemed unnecessary. I should have worn the bigger one, dammit. This is what happens when you let someone else give you the low-down on capabilities and preferences.

But I delivered the required lines with as much bluster as I could. Stella must have thought I was a little lame, though, because suddenly she was squirming up against my body, rubbing her pussy and tits against me like I was her own Italian leather sofa. "Hey," I said to Dave, "looks like your wife's hot for some fucking. Pity you ain't in any condition to bang her, being banged yourself. Maybe I could be a buddy and help you out."

"Oh, no, no," he started wailing, humping back at me so hard I almost fell over. "Don't fuck my wife, too!"

I looked at Stella and shrugged and she grinned and next thing you know, she was up on his back, straddling him and facing me. He gave this big *oooof!* sound as she settled in, big girl that she is, and spread her legs wide over his ass.

I ground my dick deep into Dave and pulled out the gloves. I was so hot for Stella right then, I wished I did have two dicks so I could have filled her up right. Or, three, just to make sure she'd have no complaints. But one was busy pronging her husband, so I greased up my hands and slid two, then three fingers up her ass with no resistance at all. She was more ready than he was—damn!

"Too bad you can't feel how tight your wife's ass is, butt boy," I informed Dave, who was panting and groaning. "Because I can. She's tight like your virgin pussy's tight and I'm gonna fuck you both until you walk funny."

Fingers up her ass and cock up his, I was in heaven, and right at that moment I didn't care that he was a dude. All I cared about was that I'd gotten all the ass in this house. *Baby, I am the ass master!* I laughed and fingered her pussy with my other hand, my hips churning like a piston. She was laughing, too, and crying out, "Fuck me, lover, fuck my tight ass," like I needed instructions. But I took the encouragement and reamed 'em both. Stella squeezed her tits and came, banging her ass down on her husband's back, almost falling right off. But I kept finger-fucking her until she finished screaming, and then I grabbed Dave by the hips and pounded into him like a jackhammer. She rolled off to one side, not graceful, but all loose, a well-fucked kind of tumble, her hair spreading against the leather of the sofa, her skin glistening with sweat and lube and come. She scrambled up next to Dave's head and cradled it, shoving his face in her tits. "Suck my tits!" she cried. "Come on, get your mouth sucking, or I'll make you suck his cock, too!"

That just about finished me. I groaned and felt my come just start way, way down low and erupt like a shaken pop bottle. I didn't just come, I exploded, cursing, my hands tight on Dave's ass. I came so hard I got dizzy, and staggered back a little. I had to steady myself while I watched Dave suck down his wife's tit and splatter his juice all down the back of the couch.

I was true to my word, and as soon as I could make myself decent, I stumbled out into the autumn air. My cock felt hot against my thigh and I ached with an intense sexual afterglow. Behind me, I'd left a husband and wife both fucked, both plea-sured; I felt like I've done my Boy Scout good deed for the day.

As for what I'll tell Stella when she asks me if I'd let Dave suck me off, I dunno. It's not like he makes me hot. But okay, maybe I'm a little more bi than I thought, if my body could react like that when I had a dude and a lady at the same time. Or maybe I am such a sucker for doing what the lady wants, someone like Stella can just get me to deliver the goods.

Either way, I think I can live with it.

PLUGGED IN

Rachel Kramer Bussel

I think I know the silver vibrating butt plug intimately—after all, I've slipped it inside Cole's ass countless times. He's a glutton for all kinds of anal penetration, and nothing makes him shiver and shake and moan like my tongue slithering inside him there—well, nothing save for this beloved toy, our favorite of our collection. It's not the most expensive toy we own—that would be the silk and rhinestone handcuffs—but this plug is special, and is about to become more special, because I've decided that I finally want it inside me.

It took me a while to get into anal sex. Receiving, that is; giving has been fun ever since the first time, with a hot dyke who showed me that it's a big myth that women aren't into being played with back there. I'd never been with anyone, guy or girl, who'd wanted to be touched in that most intimate, delicate place, and she definitely did, although it took her a while to let me know. Once she did, though, I learned to lube up my fingers or a toy and play with her in both holes, to our great enjoyment, wishing I had more hands so I could go even further. When I met Cole two years ago, we clicked right away, in and out of the bedroom. Sometimes I laugh because on the surface, he looks so preppy and proper; that's a part of his WASPy upbringing he's never quite been able to shake. No tattoos or piercings or punk-rock T-shirts for him; no board shorts or Vans or black-framed glasses or scruffy beard; he'd die if he were mistaken for a hipster. He's always clean shaven, and looks at least ten years younger than his thirty-five; he gets carded when we go to bars, but I, at thirty-one, rarely do. Yet somehow, we fit, even though I don't look anything like the blonde princesses he used to date. I have bright red hair, a combination of my natural hue with a little extra oomph, and I dress to emphasize all my curves. If I were a blonde, I'd be a bleach blonde like Anna Nicole Smith, and I'd do it, too, if I could get away with it. I have no problem being ogled, catcalled and noticed, and slowly Cole has come around to being by my side and being noticed, too.

When we started trying out toys, we used my collection; he didn't have any, although he had plenty of experience with his own and others' fingers in his ass. He wouldn't let me take him sex toy shopping, even when I promised him we'd drive a few towns over to the giant adult superstore. "Not a chance," he said, even when I straddled him and kissed him as passionately as I could. So instead, we browsed online for two hours, weighing the pros and cons of every toy we could imagine, laughing at some of the more outrageous items like cages and hoods, but eventually finding more than enough to stock our bedside drawer.

We've tried everything from dildos to padded cuffs, blindfolds to butt plugs, but it wasn't until recently, when we visited an actual toy store, that we took our relationship to a truly new level. Cole stepping out of his comfort zone made me love him even more—and want to step out of mine. Beforehand, I'd asked what he was worried about. Was it seeing someone he knew? "No, because that person would be shopping there, too. It's strangers, actually. It's like they'll know all about me from what I pick up."

"And?" I'd kissed him deeply then decided to offer a little reward for what he was sharing. I rolled him over and began massaging his cute little bubble butt, holding it open in the way that's always a prelude to penetration.

"And...they'd know I like, you know."

I couldn't help it—I laughed. "Honey, if you can't even say what it is you like, you're not gonna get very far. Say it with me: 'I like to have toys and fingers and tongues in my ass.'"

"That's not true," he said, lunging for me. "I like to have toys and *your* fingers and *your* tongue in my ass."

"Okay, I'll accept that," I'd conceded, and proceeded to put all those things in his ass, in the opposite order—tongue first, always a delight because it made him practically explode on first contact. "And maybe I'll even get something to try on me."

Cole stopped in the middle of putting his clothes on and stared at me. "You?" He couldn't have looked more stunned if I'd said I wanted to have an orgy and broadcast it on the Internet. He didn't need to complete the thought, because I could hear it loud and clear: *But you barely like a finger in your ass.* It was true, and yet I'd been thinking about it—and touching myself to those formerly forbidden thoughts. The truth was that I didn't dislike having his finger there, I just wasn't sure what was coming next, and that uncertainty made me tense up. I may look like the personification of carefree thinking, but I actually like to plan ahead, to know what's next, to anticipate it, whether we're talking sex or next week's schedule. I'm all for experimentation, but my body needs to be eased into things, just like Cole's did. My mind had been doing the prep work, apparently one step ahead of the rest of me, and my ass was responding, clenching around air when I used my favorite vibrator, tingling when I was in the shower and so much as brushed my hand back there.

Sometimes fantasies spring up seemingly out of the blue; like dreams, I'm sure they have an official explanation buried way deep down, but I didn't feel the need to investigate that closely when I could be finding out how it felt for myself. I decided to start with the most basic of beginner plugs, a slim, ridged red toy, barely wider than a finger. At the store, I dangled it in the air at him with a knowing smile. Cole had come out of his shell, energized by the prospect of playing with me there. "It really turns you on?" I asked, to be sure he wanted to try this with me and wasn't just humoring me. Even though I knew how thrilling it was for me to play with him there, I wasn't convinced it would be the same for him with me.

"I'll show you exactly how much it turns me on when we get home," he said, managing to brush against me enough to give me a hint. We didn't linger at the store, because it had done its job, providing us with the butt plug and enough foreplay that we both had to restrain ourselves from reaching into our pants on the drive home. We'd walked out with that plug, a giant bottle of lube, an extra pair of handcuffs and a blindfold; that was enough for now, and we could always go back.

"Go get ready," he grunted at me when we walked in the door; a quick peek revealed that his erection was even firmer than it had been before. There was nothing timid about his voice or his cock, just fierce lust, which made me tighten up all over. I stripped my clothes off right in the living room, leaving them in a pile on the floor as I laughed while heading into the shower. I turned the water to the hottest level I could stand, letting its warmth travel down my body as I thought about the many times Cole had grabbed me and fucked me so hard in this very shower I could feel the echoes of it well into the rest of the day. I reached behind me and held my asscheeks open, letting the spray hit me in that sensitive spot, but I could only hold that pose a few seconds. My knees were weak with arousal, and I wanted to get that plug into me.

I soaped up, rinsed off, and wrapped a fluffy white towel around me, not even bothering to wipe the film off the mirror. I knew what I looked like naked, and I wanted Cole to see me in all my warm, clean glory. I dried off, hung up the towel, then made my way upstairs. "Couldn't wait for me, huh?" I asked when I saw my husband lying on his back, slowly stroking his long, thick, very hard cock. I'm not a size queen by any means, but I do feel lucky to have wound up with a man whose entire body makes me eager to touch and taste it.

"I'm just getting ready for you to suck my cock once you have that pretty little plug inside you," he said. I joined him on the bed, not resisting my impulse to lick the head, already glistening with precome. He held my cheeks open just as I had his earlier, watching me as I circled the engorged tip with my tongue. "Okay, enough of that for now. I need to give your ass some attention."

He shifted me so I was straddling him, planting my pussy right against his hungry tongue, licking me until I almost screamed, before moving on to give my back door a similar treatment. I let out the breath I'd been holding and sank into the pleasure of his tongue teasing my puckered entrance, quick licks that soon built to big laps before he was pressing his tongue into my hole. "Oh my god," I gasped, as he upped the ante by sliding a finger into my pussy at the same time. "Yes," I murmured, already incoherent. He kept going and going, until I was almost delirious, and only then did Cole lift me off of him and seamlessly pour some lube onto his fingers and start entering me with one. I pressed back against him immediately. "Yeah, fuck my finger," he urged, and that's exactly what I did, until his finger just wasn't enough.

"You sure you're ready for this plug?" he teased, since I so clearly was.

"Very sure," I said, and soon it was inside me. "Deeper," I demanded, and he twirled the plug and pressed it more firmly against me, but right away I knew it wasn't enough. Don't get me wrong—it felt amazing, but I intuitively could tell my body was ready for more, my ass clamoring for a fuller sensation. "I want more," I said. "I want the silver plug." That's what this had all been building toward, I was sure of it, as sure as I was that I was so excited I was very likely to expel this toy by squeezing it with my newly developed anal muscles.

"Baby, that plug is pretty big. I don't know if you're up for that when you're still so new to this."

"Why don't we find out?" I panted. "You can always take it out."

"Okay..." he said, without as much certainty as I felt. "It's intense. Just to warn you."

"I like intense," I said, as he rummaged for the toy in our voluminous bedside drawer. I kept my eyes closed, the better to focus on the head of the pointed bulbous toy that would shortly be pressing against me. I knew from using it on Cole that its width and roundness was what made it a challenge, not its length. As the plug started to enter me, his fingers curled into my wetness, a dual assault. The more pressure his fingers applied, the easier it was for me to let the plug in, and when I did, I was rewarded by him turning it on. The vibrations rippled outward, upward; I felt like my whole body was vibrating.

I let out a sob, the kind you make when there are no other sounds to make, the opposite of sorrow, a sensual scream as the ripples ricocheted through me. "Go with it, baby, you've got it," he said, and he knows me well enough that instead of slamming his fingers in and out, he simply pressed them deep inside me, curving them just so, letting me know they were there. I pushed back against them, my anus tightening around the plug, which made its reverberations even stronger. The feedback loop seemed to go on forever, like looking at yourself between two mirrors, an extended reflection that never ended.

I barely realized I was rocking my hips back and forth until my head almost slipped off the pillow. "Imagine what that would feel like if I tied your legs and arms to the bedposts," he said, "and filled you up with a toy in each hole." I grunted, squeezing tighter. "Or maybe I'll tie your ankles and wrists behind your back and while you have toys in your pussy and ass I'll fuck your pretty mouth. You'd like that, wouldn't you?"

I could barely get out a "Yes," before he slid a third finger into my pussy and I buried my head in the pillow, the pressure overwhelming. I let out more sobs, the echoes of the plug's vibrations traveling all the way up and down my body as my orgasm crashed through me. His fingers seemed to expand as I tightened around him, everything intensified by being pleasured in both places at once. I sobbed, shuddered and sank into the bed as he eventually removed his fingers, turned off the plug and slid it out, which gave my body another corresponding thrill, like when nipple clamps are removed, a reminder of the pleasure the toy had already provided.

"So?" he asked with a grin. I planted my mouth on his, my tongue pressing deeply inside him. Now I knew a little bit more about what it felt like for him; the plug was another experience we could share, trading off, or even getting another one and both using them at once.

"So, now that I know how amazing that is, I can't believe I waited so long to try it."

"It's never too late to learn new things," he said. We retreated to the shower, soaping up and relearning plenty about each other's wet, slippery bodies.

ABOUT THE AUTHORS

LAURA ANTONIOU (LAntoniou.com) has been writing erotica for over twenty years. Best known for her *Marketplace* series, she has also edited and appeared in many anthologies. She has recently finished her first mystery, *The Killer Wore Leather,* and is working on book 6 of the *MP* series.

TENILLE BROWN's erotic fiction is widely published online and in nearly forty print anthologies including *Chocolate Flava 1* and *3, Curvy Girls, Making The Hook Up, Going Down, Best Bondage Erotic, 2011* and *2012, Sapphic Planet* and *Suite Encounters.* The Southern wife and mother blogs at therealtenille.com.

A world-traveling foodie, **FIONA CURTIS** now lives in the Bible Belt (hence the pseudonym), where she battles religious conservatism with sauciness.

KATE DOMINIC is a former technical writer who now writes about more interesting ways to put tabs into slots. She is the author of over four hundred erotic short stories, which have been published under many names and in several languages. She is currently studying medieval illuminated manuscripts and working on a historical novel.

EMERALD's erotic fiction has been published in anthologies such as *Please, Sir* and *Best Women's Erotica 2010* as well as at various erotic websites. She may be found online at her website, thegreenlightdistrict.org. Las Vegas is one of her favorite places.

EROBINTICA (erobintica.blogspot.com) is poet, writer and blogger Robin Elizabeth Sampson. She's been published in *Coming Together: Al Fresco, Best Erotic Romance, Best Erotic Romance 2013, Suite Encounters: Hotel Sex Stories* and *Ageless Erotica*.

SHOSHANNA EVERS (shoshanna.evers@yahoo.com) writes erotic romance for Ellora's Cave and Berkley Heat. In addition to writing, Shoshanna is a registered nurse, advice columnist, wife and mother.

D. FOSTALOVE lives in Atlanta, Georgia, where he is currently at work on several projects, including a follow-up to *Unraveled: Sealed Lips, Clenched Fists*.

M. HOWARD enjoys exploring the human condition through adult fiction. His work was widely featured in the ground-breaking online weekly, Ruthie's Club, and has been featured in *Justus Roux Erotic Tales* and Tinder James's anthology, *Stretched*.

D. L. KING's (dlkingerotica.blogspot.com) short stories have appeared in titles such as *Luscious, Hurts So Good, One Night Only, Please, Ma'am* and many others. She is the editor of *Under Her Thumb, Seductress, The Harder She Comes, Spankalicious, Carnal Machines, Spank!, The Sweetest Kiss* and *Where the Girls Are.*

ANNABETH LEONG's (annabethleong.blogspot.com) recent work includes a meditation on fellatio insecurities in *Going Down: Oral Sex Stories* and a violet-scented lesbian romance in *Like Hearts Enchanted.* Annabeth loves freedom of speech, shoes, cooking and music. She lives in Providence, Rhode Island.

ANYA LEVIN is the author of numerous erotic short stories, most of which star fearless women who aren't afraid to go after whatever—and whoever—they desire. Her work has appeared in numerous anthologies, including *Girl Fever, Gotta Have It* and *Mammoth Book of Best New Erotica 11.*

MEDEA MOR's (medea-mor.tumblr.com) short stories have been published in several recent Cleis anthologies. She hopes soon to publish a Victorian BDSM novel entitled *The Seduction of Lucy Deane*, as well as a short-story collection.

MAGGIE MORTON lives in Northern California with her partner and their Japanese Bobtail. Her stand-alone stories *Julie Repents* and *From Top to Bottom* are published by Ravenous Romance, and her novel *Dreaming of Her*, a lesbian erotic romance, is published by Bold Strokes Books.

MINA MURRAY (minamurray.wordpress.com) is a whisky aficionado and smut-peddler who can often be found with her head in a book. Her work will appear in the forthcoming volumes *Seductress: Erotic Tales of Immortal Desire* and *Best Bondage Erotica 2013.*

TIFFANY REISZ lives in Lexington, Kentucky, where she can often be found making up dirty bedtime stories and annoying her cats and boyfriend when she should be cleaning the bathroom. She is the author of *The Original Sinners* series (*The Siren, The Angel, The Prince*) from MIRA Books.

Eroticist **GISELLE RENARDE** (wix.com/gisellerenarde/erotica) is a queer Canadian, avid volunteer, contributor to more than fifty short-story anthologies, and author of dozens of electronic and print books, including *Anonymous, Ondine* and *My Mistress' Thighs.* Ms. Renarde lives across from a park with two bilingual cats who sleep on her head.

TALON RIHAI AND **SALOME WILDE's** coauthored publications include stories in Rachel Kramer Bussel's *Anything for You* and *Curvy Girls.* Their gay romance novella *After the First Taste of Love* is forthcoming from Storm Moon Press. Wilde has published many stories solo, in anthologies by Susie Bright, Maxim Jakubowski, and Rachel Kramer Bussel.

THOMAS S. ROCHE's novel, *The Panama Laugh,* was a finalist for the Horror Writers' Association's Bram Stoker Award. Roche's other books include the *Noirotica* series of erotic crime anthologies and four collections of fantasy and horror. A prolific blogger, Roche writes regularly for TinyNibbles.com, Boiled-Hard.com and many other blogs.

ANGELA R. SARGENTI is currently hard at work on her latest novel. Her work appears in such anthologies as *Best Bondage Erotica 2012, Spankalicious* and *Anything For You.* She has two e-books of her own, *Working Out the Kinks* and *Start Me Up: A Collection of Erotic Love Stories.*

KATHLEEN TUDOR's (KathleenTudor.com) work has appeared in *Anything for You: Erotica for Kinky Couples, Best Bondage Erotica 2012, Hot Under the Collar* and other anthologies. She is also coeditor of the Circlet Press anthology, *Like Hearts Enchanted.*

VERONICA WILDE (veronicawilde.com) is an erotic romance author whose work has been published by Cleis Press, Bella Books, Xcite Books, Liquid Silver Books and Samhain Publishing.

ABOUT
THE EDITOR

RACHEL KRAMER BUSSEL (rachelkramerbussel.com) is a New York–based author, editor and blogger. She has edited over forty books of erotica, including *Anything for You; The Big Book of Orgasms; Suite Encounters; Going Down; Irresistible; Gotta Have It; Obsessed; Women in Lust; Surrender; Orgasmic; Cheeky Spanking Stories; Bottoms Up; Spanked: Red-Cheeked Erotica; Fast Girls; Smooth; Passion; The Mile High Club; Do Not Disturb; Going Down; Tasting Him; Tasting Her; Please, Sir; Please, Ma'am; He's on Top; She's on Top; Caught Looking; Hide and Seek; Crossdressing; Rubber Sex,* and is *Best Sex Writing* series editor. Her anthologies have won 8 IPPY (Independent Publisher) Awards, and *Surrender* won the National Leather Association Samois Anthology Award. Her work has been published in over one hundred anthologies, including *Best American Erotica 2004* and *2006*. She wrote the popular "Lusty Lady" column for the *Village Voice*.

Rachel has written for *AVN, Bust,* Cleansheets.com, *Cosmo-*

politan, Curve, The Daily Beast, TheFrisky.com, *Glamour,* Gothamist, Huffington Post, *Inked,* Mediabistro, *Newsday, New York Post, New York Observer, Penthouse,* The Root, Salon, *San Francisco Chronicle, Time Out New York* and *Zink,* among others. She has appeared on "The Gayle King Show," "The Martha Stewart Show," "The Berman and Berman Show," NY1 and Showtime's "Family Business." She hosted the popular In the Flesh Erotic Reading Series (inthefleshreadingseries.com), featuring readers from Susie Bright to Zane, and speaks at conferences, does readings and teaches erotic writing workshops across the country. She blogs at lustylady.blogspot.com.

More from Rachel Kramer Bussel

Do Not Disturb
Hotel Sex Stories
Edited by Rachel Kramer Bussel

A delicious array of hotel hookups where it seems like anything can happen—and quite often does. "If *Do Not Disturb* were a hotel, it would be a 5-star hotel with the luxury of 24/7 entertainment available."—Erotica Revealed
978-1-57344-344-9 $14.95

Bottoms Up
Spanking Good Stories
Edited by Rachel Kramer Bussel

As sweet as it is kinky, *Bottoms Up* will propel you to pick up a paddle and share in both pleasure and pain, or perhaps simply turn the other cheek.
ISBN 978-1-57344-362-3 $15.95

Orgasmic
Erotica for Women
Edited by Rachel Kramer Bussel

What gets you off? Let *Orgasmic* count the ways...with 25 stories focused on female orgasm, there is something here for every reader.
ISBN 978-1-57344-402-6 $14.95

Please, Sir
Erotic Stories of Female Submission
Edited by Rachel Kramer Bussel

These 22 kinky stories celebrate the thrill of submission by women who know exactly what they want.
ISBN 978-1-57344-389-0 $14.95

Fast Girls
Erotica for Women
Edited by Rachel Kramer Bussel

Fast Girls celebrates the girl with a reputation, the girl who goes all the way, and the girl who doesn't know how to say "no."
ISBN 978-1-57344-384-5 $14.95

Many More Than Fifty Shades of Erotica

Please, Sir
Erotic Stories of Female Submission
Edited by Rachel Kramer Bussel

If you liked *Fifty Shades of Grey,* you'll love the explosive stories of *Yes, Sir.* These damsels delight in the pleasures of taking risks to be rewarded by the men who know their deepest desires. Find out why nothing is as hot as the power of the words "Please, Sir."
ISBN 978-1-57344-389-0 $14.95

Yes, Sir
Erotic Stories of Female Submission
Edited by Rachel Kramer Bussel

Bound, gagged or spanked—or controlled with just a glance—these lucky women experience the breathtaking thrills of sexual submission. *Yes, Sir* shows that pleasure is best when dispensed by a firm hand.
ISBN 978-1-57344-310-4 $15.95

He's on Top
Erotic Stories of Male Dominance and Female Submission
Edited by Rachel Kramer Bussel

As true tops, the bossy hunks in these stories understand that BDSM is about exulting in power that is freely yielded. These kinky stories celebrate women who know exactly what they want.
ISBN 978-1-57344-270-1 $14.95

Best Bondage Erotica 2012
Edited by Rachel Kramer Bussel

How do you want to be teased, tied and tantalized? Whether you prefer a tough top with shiny handcuffs, the tug of rope on your skin or the sound of your lover's command, Rachel Kramer Bussel serves your needs.
ISBN 978-1-57344-754-6 $15.95

Luscious
Stories of Anal Eroticism
Edited by Alison Tyler

Discover all the erotic possibilities that exist between the sheets and between the cheeks in this daring collection. "Alison Tyler is an author to rely on for steamy, sexy page turners! Try her!"—Powell's Books
ISBN 978-1-57344-760-7 $15.95

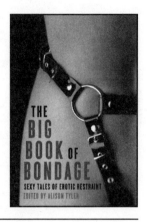

Ordering is easy! Call us toll free or fax us to place your MC/VISA order.
You can also mail the order form below with payment to:
Cleis Press, 2246 Sixth St., Berkeley, CA 94710.

ORDER FORM

QTY	TITLE	PRICE
____	_____	_____
____	_____	_____
____	_____	_____
____	_____	_____
____	_____	_____
____	_____	_____
____	_____	_____

SUBTOTAL _____

SHIPPING _____

SALES TAX _____

TOTAL _____

Add $3.95 postage/handling for the first book ordered and $1.00 for each additional book. Outside North America, please contact us for shipping rates. California residents add 9% sales tax. Payment in U.S. dollars only.

* Free book of equal or lesser value. Shipping and applicable sales tax extra.

Cleis Press • Phone: (800) 780-2279 • Fax: (510) 845-8001
orders@cleispress.com • www.cleispress.com
You'll find more great books on our website

Follow us on Twitter @cleispress • Friend/fan us on Facebook